STALKER

Cyborg Ranger

Clarissa Lake
Christine Myers

Contains Sexually Explicit Scenes

Clarissa Lake's Other works:

Szeqart Prison Planet Series
Soliv Four
Coraz

Narovian Mates Series
Dream Alien
Alien Alliances
Her Alien Captain
Her Alien Trader

Farseek Mercenary Series
Commander's Mate
Lieutenant's Mate
Sahvin's Mate
Argen's Mate
Faigon's Mate

Farseek Warrior Series
Kragyn
Narzek
Roran

Wicked Ways

Interstellar Matchmaking
Korjh's Bride
Rader's Bride
Joven's Bride

with Christine Myers
Jolt Somber
Talia's Cyborg

Cyborg Ranger Series
Blaze, Cyborg Ranger
Darken, Cyborg Ranger

https://amazon.com/author/clarissalake
https://amazon.com/author/christinemyers

Please keep in touch. Visit my website and sign up for my newsletter at: http://clarissalake.authors.zone/.

Everyone who signs up will get a free book.

Contents

Chapter One

Cyborg Stalker Knight and his four brothers in arms gathered in the woods where they'd left their sky cycles. They'd just finished their mission to help Ranger Captain Savage rescue his wife from an Eastern overlord. It was the most excitement they'd had since they'd returned to Earth a few months before.

Darken Wolf reached his sky-cycle first, and Stalker couldn't help overhearing the conversation he was having with his wife.

"Don't worry, Gina. I'm not going to land. It's just a flyover."

"Hey, Darken," said Stalker. "Want some company? We don't have anything pressing. I wouldn't mind killing a few more goons."

"Hear that, baby? I've got back up."

Gina sighed. "Okay, that makes me feel better, but I will never forgive you if you get yourself killed."

Darken laughed. "Don't worry, love. I'm not that easy to kill. Many have tried, and I am still here."

"Come back to me. That's all I ask."

"That's my plan, sweetheart."

"I love you."

"And I love you." Darken broke the connection. He would not say goodbye.

"You and the captain are lucky bastards," said Stalker. "What I wouldn't give for a female of my own."

"It could still happen; they get new profiles into the system every day. Captain Savage found his own."

"You going rogue, Darken?" Shadow Hawk asked.

"Not rogue. This is tied into Gina's kidnapping and the disappearance of people from my territory." Darken told them about Gina tying Wayne Stockman to Devlin White.

"Oh, yeah. Count me in," said Max Steel followed by Falcon Rader. It was unanimous.

"We've got nothing better to do. It might be fun," said Falcon."

They all mounted their sky cycles and headed north to the coordinates Darken had shared with them.

Sky cycles were mechanical shape shifting vehicles. They operated in three related configurations—a hovering motorcycle, flying motorcycle with wings extended, and a personal flyer with a complete cockpit enclosing the riders.

The five cyborgs traveled at breakneck speed in flyer mode and reached Devlin's compound in about half an hour. They did several flyovers, scanning and recording what they saw. Like the one in the desert, a new Quonset hut had been added since Darken's last visit there to rescue Gina. It sat toward the edge of the property, away from the mansion at the compound's center, housing about a hundred people. Beside it, the missing transport was parked.

Darken knew it was the same vehicle because he recognized its electronic signature when he pinged it. He'd only hovered above it for seconds when an ion rifle bolt whizzed by his head. Only it was no ordinary ion rifle. It was a stationary ion repeater mounted on one of four towers.

They know we're here. Let's go! As eager as his cohorts were for action, Darken reminded them they had no jurisdiction. This was strictly recon.

Only, just as Darken was about to gun his throttle, two bolts hit him in the back. Max and Stalker pulled their rifles and took out the shooter and the whole tower.

16

Holding on to consciousness by a thread, Darken sped away into the night, and the other four team members followed. They made it to the mountains in Enclave Territory before Darken's cycle landed, and he fell to the ground, landing flat on his back, unconscious.

Stalker was the first to reach him, while the other three landed nearby. A quick scan of Darken's diagnostics revealed severe damage to his right lung, left kidney, and liver.

Stalker opened the emergency pack on his belt and shot a full bolus of auxiliary nanites up Darken's nose. He took out a second bolus, turned his friend over, and pumped more nanites into the gaping wounds. Had Darken not been in full armor, he would probably be dead.

As things stood, Darken had lost a lot of blood, enough to render him unconscious.

"We need to get him out of here. I tapped into one of our satellites, and flyers are heading this way," said Max.

"Help me get him on his cycle and strap him on it. I'll set it to fly him home, then we'll take care of the flyers."

Easy money, Neely Albert thought as she sent her Class Two flyer upward vertically. Fly a cargo hold of ion rifles an hour and fifteen minutes south of Farringay, unload and fly back. It was probably not legal, but she was doing it anyway.

Payment for this run would give her enough money to move West out of overlord territory. Alexander Berke would be paid off for the repair of her flyer. She planned to leave after she got the hover plane from her father, but it needed a major overhaul.

Neely went to Berke for a loan, and he gave her two choices. She could either go back to work in the brothel or fly for him once the plane was repaired. Neely chose the latter. She was done whoring for Alexander Berke.

He had a nice racket for himself. By paying them a set rate for their services, Berke then charged them for everything so that they made only a pittance above their expenses. They were protected in his compound from the gangers in the city ruins, but they might as well be in prison.

It was a beautiful night for a flight. The sky was clear and filled with stars and a quarter moon. Neely loved being in the quiet serenity when it was like this. Her time in the air seemed to end too quickly as she neared the drop coordinates.

Berke had assured her that cyborg Colton Price was expecting her. She would land at the overlord's compound, and he would take delivery.

Only when she slowed her approach to hover and land, someone started shooting and hitting her plane.

"Price! What the fuck?" she yelled into the com as she banked her flyer left and flew off to the west. The next thing she knew, two armed flyers were on her tail. She maxed out her speed and zigzagged as much as possible to avoid getting hit, but it didn't work.

The engine took a hit, and her flyer was going down smoking. The emergency harness held her fast in the pilot seat as Neely slowed her descent as much as she could without engine power. Even then, she was pretty sure she was going to die. The ground was coming up way too fast.

The plane hit nose first, and airbags deployed. At least dead, Neely would have no more worries about the future, she thought just before everything went black.

Two flyers came their way only minutes after they sent Darken on his way, one in pursuit of the other. The cyborgs quickly determined that one was pursuing the other as the one behind was firing ahead. The flyer in front had a human pilot while the pursuer was a cyborg not on their internal net.

That meant he was a natural convert, a natural-born human converted to a cyborg to repair catastrophic war injuries. Not all of them were enemies, but many had gone rogue after the war and allied themselves with the overlords.

They used their ion rifles to shoot down the pursuers, but not before the front flyer took a hit. Seeing that it was headed for a crash landing, Max and Stalker slung their rifles over their shoulders and ran for their sky cycles. The flyer had crashed a little over a mile away. The battered wreck was smoking when they landed about fifty yards away, and the two cyborgs ran to free the pilot. With airbags and a safety harness, he probably lived through the crash.

When the butterfly door wouldn't open, Stalker punched out the window, and Max helped him rip the whole door off. The flyer's engine compartment started to flame. There was no time for finesse. Stalker ripped the harness away from the pilot, pulled him out, slung him over his shoulder, and ran toward the cycles.

The flyer exploded, spewing engine parts and cargo out the back. A change in wind direction stoked the flames toward the cockpit. Stalker carried the pilot another fifty yards further from the wreck, signaling his sky cycle to follow. He knelt on the ground, cradling the pilot over his lap.

Carefully removing the pilot's helmet, "A female," he rasped in surprise. He glanced up at Max, then back at her. "*My* female."

Mentally shaking himself, Stalker started scanning her for injuries, thankful she was at least breathing. Apparently, the harness and airbag saved her life. However, the speed and the sudden stop caused bruises from the restraint on the outside, internal damage, and a significant concussion, but no brain bleed. Stalker reached for a bolus of nanites from a pouch on his belt. With her head cradled against his forearm, he uncapped it and squirted it up her nose.

"What do you think they wanted with her?" Max wondered.

"Maybe they thought she was with us." Stalker turned his head as he caught a movement in his peripheral vision. "Someone's coming... The cyborg convert...."

Max ran to his cycle and yanked his ion rifle from its sling. Raising it to his shoulder, he moved to a spot between his friend and the male approaching. When the cyborg came closer, Max demanded, "who are you, and what do you want?"

"Colton Price. I came to see that the pilot got out of the flyer after it crashed and to find out why he was flying over Overlord White's compound."

"The pilot is female... My female and she is unconscious."

"So, she was with you?"

Stalker wanted to say yes, but it was an outright lie. Manufactured cyborgs were incapable of direct lies. "I can't tell you that. We were investigating a series of kidnappings in old Texas and New Mexico."

Stalker surmised from Colton's expression that the natural convert knew he was evading the question. As a war veteran, he would know that no manufactured cyborg could lie in answering a direct question. He

22

would also know that Stalker would fight to the death for *his* female.

"Since she was the pilot, she is not the person we were after," said Colton cryptically. "Now, I have to go back and tell the boss why we lost a drone, and my flyer is wrecked. You and your female should probably make yourselves scarce. I'm sure we'll meet again." As he spoke, he turned and started walking away.

Chapter Two

Twenty minutes later, the pilot still hadn't regained consciousness, but Stalker's repeat scan told him her vitals were stable.

"Max, I've got this. You can be on your way. I'm just going to give her a little more time to regain consciousness, then we'll be leaving."

"If you are sure…. If anything deviates from your projection, call me on our net."

"Thanks, I will." Stalker nodded. "I'll let you know how things turn out."

As Max flew off on his sky cycle, Stalker studied his female's face, amazed at how she so closely matched the avatar he'd known in his virtual life in stasis. The only major difference was that the avatar had long brown hair, whereas his actual female had short-cropped brown hair tipped in bright red and piercings in her nose and ears with small silver rings. Her facial shape, mouth, nose, and cheekbones were like the avatar.

She was the most beautiful woman he had ever seen in his eyes. He so wished she would wake. He wanted to know everything about her…. To kiss her soft full lips and hold her in his arms… To strip her bare and worship every inch of her body with his lips and tongue.

His cock went hard as he just thought about breeding her. Only, he knew that she might have other ideas. Just because she looked like the avatar didn't mean she would instantly accept him as her mate. They had all been warned that their genetic mate would not adhere to the behavior of the avatar mate.

Since she hadn't regained consciousness, Stalker got up, lifting her in his arms, deciding he needed to find shelter where she could rest and recover. Someone else could come along to make trouble before his female awakened.

His home outside Los Angeles ruins was on the other side of the country. Stalker carried her to his sky cycle and harnessed her in the passenger seat, then he picked up her helmet and stowed it in the cargo compartment. He took his seat in front and converted the vehicle into a mini-flyer complete with a closed cockpit.

Sending it straight up into the air, he headed west above the treetops for about fifteen minutes, scanning for an unoccupied house that could shelter them while his female recovered. He found an empty farmhouse by an old road with some windows intact and no neighbors nearby.

Stalker set the cycle down by a side porch one step up from the ground. Extracting the woman from the bike, he carried her inside through an old kitchen and into a sitting room containing a couple of stuffed chairs and a ragged sofa. Everything was covered in a layer of dust. Balancing her over his shoulder, he took a small cylinder from his pouch belt. As he opened it, a tab popped out so he could pull out the compressed plastic blanket within. Spreading it over the couch, he laid his female on top of it.

Stalker secured his cycle from his internal computer and paced the room while he rescanned her because she was not waking up. Cross-referencing the result of his scan with medical protocol internally, he determined another bolus of nanites might help and definitely wouldn't hurt.

After giving her the second nanite bolus, Stalker sat in the chair perpendicular to the sofa so he could watch her. He was too anxious and excited to rest, alternating between sitting and pacing and rescanning her to gauge her recovery progress.

Every minute seemed like an hour, although each scan showed improvement.

Meanwhile, Stalker contacted Captain Savage and the other team members to let them know he'd found his genetic mate. That was a formality to let them know he needed time to work out a relationship with her.

He paused in his pacing and stood by the sofa, looking down at her. Unable to help himself, Stalker bent to stroke her smooth cheek with his fingers. The woman sucked in a breath and opened her eyes with a start as he touched her.

"What are you doing? Who are you?" She struggled to sit up, so Stalker hunkered down and helped her, gripping her forearm and slipping his hand behind her back.

"Waiting for you to regain consciousness. I just wanted to see if your skin was as smooth and soft as it looked," he told her honestly.

"Who the hell are you, and why did you shoot down my flyer?" She started to get up and lost her balance as she stood, falling back on the couch.

"Wow, so dizzy," she muttered.

"We didn't shoot you down; it was the flyer behind you. We shot him down."

"Where is my flyer? I have to get the cargo out." she struggled, trying to get up again.

"Sh, sh, sh. Take it easy. You have a concussion and were shaken up pretty good." He squatted in front of her to be closer to eye level. "I am Stalker Knight, your cyborg."

"What!? What do you mean?"

"You are my genetic mate, the one female I can breed and make a family with."

"Oh, I don't think so," she asserted. "I'm not anyone's breeder, and I don't even know you."

Stalker sighed. He should have known it couldn't be that easy. Darken was lucky. His female had asked for a cyborg mate, so she accepted to bond with him right away.

"I understand that getting to know me will take time," he said, meeting her gaze. "I'm sorry to tell you; your flyer is a total loss. It was on fire when it crashed, and I pulled you out just before it exploded and finished burning up. Whatever you were carrying was destroyed as well."

"How do I know that you aren't just saying that?"

"I can't lie. Everything was recorded on my internal computer." Stalker stood and took out a small computer tablet. Sitting beside her on the sofa, he brought up the hologram of the crash starting where her plane was hit."

"Omigod, they're going to kill me," she murmured.

"Why, what were you carrying?"

"Guns...Ion rifles."

"For who?"

"I can't tell you that. I am in enough trouble."

"No one is going to hurt you. They will have to go through me, and I am not so easy to kill. Many have tried." He paused, putting his arm behind her on the back of the couch. "Will you at least tell me your name?"

She took a breath, scowling at him. "Neely Albert."

"Neely, I am a law enforcement ranger for the Civil Restoration Enclave, which governs the territory from the Appalachians west. I will help you any way I can, but I need to know what's going on. Who were the rifles for?"

Neely pressed her lips together in a thin line, frowning at him for several moments.

"Overlords Edmund Stone and Devlin White," she said finally.

"Problem solved."

"What do you mean?"

"He's dead. Captain Savage killed him yesterday."

"What about his cyborgs? One of them gave me the order... Colton Price."

"Then, he probably shouldn't have shot down your flyer. He walked up to the site after we shot his flyer down, and he saw that you were the pilot he shot down."

"What the hell did he do that for?"

"No clue. He just said you weren't who he was after. We decided he was after us instead."

"That doesn't make any sense. He knows the electronic signature of my craft. Price doesn't make that kind of mistake."

"It doesn't seem logical to me either. But until Price shot you down, we thought all three of you were after us. Then we shot him and the drone down. Give me a minute while I check his records.

"He is a converted natural from devastating injuries in the war, which I expected. His wife Tessa was taken while he was recovering and sold at an illegal human trafficking auction. Colton went berserk after he found out, and he was discharged back to Earth just before the war ended."

"Well, that would explain why he is such an asshole," she muttered.

"How so?"

"Moody and angry. Other times he doesn't seem to give a crap. But he goes out of his way to cater to all the Overlords."

"Since the overlords are behind most human trafficking, that's a logical move. He's trying to find her by infiltrating the Overlords' operations."

"I still don't understand why he would shoot me down."

"Maybe to slow us down to find out what we were doing at Overlord White's compound.

"What were you doing?"

"Recon. People were kidnapped from the villages out west, and we were trying to find out who was doing it."

"They are all involved…."

31

"And technically, we are not supposed to enter their territory. The Overlords have a treaty with the Enclave, but they broke it first, taking people we are sworn to protect."

The Overlords rose to power in the aftermath of the Mesaarkans bombing every major city on Earth. They gathered all the remaining resources in the cities and rationed them, bartering for services. Gangers were their enforcers and laborers, and the Overlords were not benevolent rulers. They were tyrannical dictators. The most powerful, Alexander Berke had connections in the Federation High Council, someone influential enough to limit the Enclave reach to west of the Appalachians.

However, the Overlords had no qualms about covertly raiding Enclave territories to kidnap people and steal whatever they desired.

Chapter Three

"What good is a treaty if both sides are breaking it?" Neely asked, trying to inch away from him as he moved closer to her. His unique scent filled her nostrils, a subtle spicy musk that was intoxicating. The flutter between her thighs startled her, something that rarely happened.

Stalker leaned toward her, and she leaned away, but had nowhere to go because she was sitting against the armrest. His face was only inches from hers, and he was staring at her lips. She started to lean toward him but turned her head and jumped up off the sofa.

A wave of dizziness hit her, and she staggered, trying to maintain her balance. Along with the dizziness, her whole head was throbbing. Her stomach was starting to feel queasy as well.

Then Stalker was in front of her, grasping her upper arms to steady her. He steered Neely back to the couch. "Here, sit down. You have a concussion. You need more rest while the nanites finish repairing the damage. Stay here, and I will get you some water off my sky bike."

Neely moaned her ascent and leaned her head back, closing her eyes against the spinning room. He was back in less than a minute with two water bottles and a couple of wrapped bars. She didn't realize he was back until she felt the cushions shift as he sat down beside her. She opened her eyes to find him holding a plastic bottle of water in front of her.

"Here's a meal bar in case you are hungry."

Accepting the bar and the water, Neely drank several swallows. She couldn't remember when she last had some. Dehydration could make her feel lightheaded and queasy. She wasn't quite ready for food.

She hated feeling weak, especially with this cyborg ranger who could do anything he wanted with her, and she wouldn't be able to stop him. Would she even want to?

Glancing at him, she couldn't deny he was incredibly attractive. All bulging muscles, sandy hair, and midnight blue eyes with soft-looking full lips. And he smelled so damn good. It was all too easy to imagine fucking him.

It had been a long time since she got laid by a male she enjoyed. She felt her cheeks heat at the turn of her thoughts, and she frowned. The last thing she should do is encourage this guy. She would never get rid of him.

"Neely, look at me," Stalker said.

She hesitated, then turned her head to look at his face.

"I don't know how much you know about cyborgs, but nothing will happen that you don't want. It is not in me to do anything deliberately that would hurt you."

She stared into his eyes, wishing something there would give her a reason not to believe him. There wasn't.

"Even if I believe that it doesn't mean I want to be your breeder. I don't want to be anyone's breeder or mate. I don't want to be tied down like that," she asserted. "I'm a smuggler and sometimes a spy. I don't stay in any one place for very long."

"It doesn't have to be that way." Stalker reached up and stroked her cheek with his fingertips. "Your flyer got shot down because you were in the wrong place at the wrong time. You won't be much of a smuggler without transport."

His tone was gentle as his caress on her face. Why did he have to be so damn sexy? How could one cyborg male be so intoxicating that her nipples tightened and her core clenched at his slight touch?

Neely had an intense urge to straddle his lap and rub herself against him. Just as intense was the urge to jump up and put some distance between them. Only she had already tried that and nearly fell on her butt.

"What have you done to me? I never feel like this around a man. You are all trouble that I don't need," she said, pushing his hand away from her face.

"You mean because you are aroused?"

She huffed and said, "No—"

"You are. I can smell your arousal."

Of course, he can. He is a cyborg. All of his senses are enhanced. Neely looked away, feeling the heat rise in her cheeks.

"Neely, it's not your fault." He applied his fingers lightly to her cheek, coaxing her to meet his gaze. "We are genetic mates; our pheromones make us want to breed. It's biological…. At least for you, it is. Cyborgs are programmed to love our genetic mate in our virtual lives before awakening. I interacted with an avatar that looks very much like you."

"You mean I don't have a choice?" Her eyes filled with angry tears. This time she got up slowly. She needed to think, and she couldn't think clearly so close to the cyborg playing havoc with her libido.

"I'm the one who has no choice. It's you or nobody. If you reject me, there will never be anyone else. That's how we are made." He paused. "We fought throughout the galaxy for the promise of a mate to love and make a family with. Every time we got hurt, they patched us up and sent us out again. We all did it for her, the genetic mate we were promised at the end of the fighting. It was an empty promise. The people who made it were dead by the time the war was over."

Neely let out an ironic laugh. "From what I know of history, that's not surprising. People in government promise you anything to make you do what they want. I'm sorry, I just don't think I can be that woman for you."

"Doesn't it make you curious about the life we could have together, given the attraction you feel?"

Neely turned away and looked out the dirty window as the sun peeked over the horizon in the distance. Was she curious? It was too easy to picture herself naked with him pounding into her until they were both sated. Even with her head still throbbing, she couldn't get it out of her mind.

She just wished she could go home to her tiny flat in the Farringay Starport City and be alone. Yet, she couldn't. Her cargo was destroyed, and Overlord Berke wouldn't get his money for the rifles she was on her way to deliver. Nor could she return them because fucking Colton Price destroyed her flyer with them inside.

It wouldn't matter if she reported it to Berke. He would expect her to work it off in one of his brothels. She'd rather take her chances with the cyborg. Neely was done using sex to get by a long time ago. She was enraged at Price for shooting down her flyer for what it cost her to get it in the first place.

That little cargo plane was her independence. Now she had nothing but the few clothes left in her furnished flat. She wouldn't risk getting caught by Berke's gangers to go back and get them.

Brushing the tears from her eyes, she turned back to face Stalker. "I want to see it. I want to see the burnt wreck of my flyer."

"You don't believe me?"

"That's not it. I just need to see it… I guess to say 'goodbye.' That flyer was the only thing I owned that was worth anything."

"Okay." Stalker quickly folded up the plastic blanket small enough to stow in his cargo compartment. "I'll take you. It's not far."

His liked the sky cycle for its versatility that allowed him to travel over any landscape whether or not there were roads where he wanted to go. For this trip, he just extended the wings so he could fly higher over the landscape.

Most of the cyborgs didn't wear helmets because their skulls were steel alloy reinforced. Not so for a normal human.

Stalker pulled Neely's helmet out of the compartment where he stowed the plastic blanket. "You were wearing this when I pulled you out. You probably should wear it; in case we get into trouble."

She nodded and took it from him while he climbed on the cycle. He waited for her to climb on behind him before starting the engine. A harness slithered out from the backrest to secure Neely on the seat.

CLARISSA LAKE · CHRISTINE MYERS

She was glad to wear the helmet because it blocked out his scent playing havoc with her libido. If he were anyone but a cyborg, she might just fuck him to get him out of her system. But she had no idea how to fight the genetics in play.

Chapter Four

They reached the crash site in fifteen minutes, and Stalker landed his sky cycle beside it. Although heavily charred, Neely could tell it was indeed her flyer. The rear cargo compartment that sat directly over the engine was completely gone, along with the ten ion rifles.

Neely walked a wide circle around the wreck, and none of the pieces of metal and plastic were identifiable. "Damn you, Colton Price!" she yelled, ending with a sob. Angry tears ran down her cheeks.

Stalker came to stand in front of her. He wanted nothing more than to hold her and soothe her tears away. "I'm sorry. Your plane was already going down when he got in range for us to shoot him down."

"I don't get it," she sniffed. "Price knows my flyer, and he knew I was taking weapons to Stone."

Stalker frowned. He and the other two cyborgs figured she was just in the wrong place at the wrong time. If Price knew plane and her mission and shot her down anyway, he meant to stop her from delivering the guns. Was he a double agent playing both sides of the fence?

"If he knew it, was you, he shot down your plane on purpose, not by mistake."

"But we both work for the Overlords…."

"And he stopped you from making your delivery to the overlord." Stalker finished.

"Are you saying he's a spy?"

"I can only speculate based on his actions. Cyborg Command didn't give me any more than I told you." Stalker rested his hands on her shoulders. "I'm sorry you lost your plane," he said gently, but he was not sorry she had to stop smuggling to the overlords.

Neely wiped the tears from her eyes. "Damn it, I hate crying. I am just so angry."

"I see that." Stalker paused and looked into her eyes, glancing at her parted lips. He wanted to kiss her so badly. "Smuggling is no life for you. You could have died in the explosion if we hadn't pulled you out."

He held her face between his hands. "You could come to California and work for me at Protector rate…."

"I barely even know you. You're a law enforcer, and I am a law breaker. How is that going to work?"

Stalker sensed she was about to pull back from him, so he kissed her. He caressed her lips gently at first, then ran the tip of his tongue between her lips. Neely hesitated, so Stalker teased her with butterfly kisses until she reached up and held his head, kissing him back in earnest.

Neely never said she didn't want him. Being close to him was driving her crazy. She worried about encouraging him. She knew he wanted forever, and she didn't know if she could give him that. She was used to looking out for herself and didn't normally do relationships.

She opened her mouth to his tongue, swirling her tongue around his. Delicious sensations rippled through her body, making her nipples and clit throb with want. Neely wasn't quite sure whether she pressed her body against his or whether he pulled her against him. He felt wonderful, and she felt wanton and impetuous.

Kissing him back would only encourage him. Yet she couldn't find it in herself to pull back… To deny herself the pleasure of his embrace. She wound her arms around his neck, caressing his head.

He lifted her off the ground so they were chest to chest, squeezing her breasts against his hard muscles and pressing her throbbing pussy against his hard cock. She wrapped her legs around him loosely, willing herself not to grind her mons against his erection.

Neely had been kissed before but never with *his* attention to her pleasure. And she found herself responding in kind. Her whole body was trembling with need when Stalker finally pulled his lips from hers. She moaned a sigh, tempted to pull him back in for another kiss.

"Yeah, oh…. Wow," she murmured, staring into his midnight blue eyes.

"I've been waiting my whole life to do that," he said, smiling. "I want to do that again, but we should leave before we're discovered."

Neely unwrapped her legs from around him, and he lowered her until her feet were on the ground again.

"Where are we going?"

"I need to get back to California. That's my assigned territory."

"That's far, isn't it?"

"Yes, and this sky cycle isn't that fast. It will take about six hours."

"Did you fly all that way in one trip?" she wondered.

"Yes, and I am planning to fly back in one trip as well," he said. "Is there a problem?"

"All I have are the clothes I am wearing. Not that I have a lot more at my flat in Starport City." He already knew why she couldn't go back there.

"Don't worry. We can stop in New Chicago and get some things you will need."

"I don't need much… a couple of outfits, a jacket, and grooming supplies." She took a step back to put some distance between them to give her a chance to recover her control. "You can take it out of my pay."

"That's not necessary…."

"For me, it is. I will take the job but don't think this means I am going to be your mate. …Not that you are unattractive. Circumstances put me in a tough spot. I'd rather take my chances with you than Alexander Berke and his gangers."

"But you want me." He gave her a sexy smirk as he said it.

"Don't get too cocky. We don't always get what we want." She gave him a meaningful look and then made the mistake of glancing at the prominent bulge at his crotch. *And we don't always want what's good for us.*

Neely turned abruptly and strode back to Stalker's sky cycle. Stalker followed, smiling to himself. With Neely already seated, Stalker swung his leg up over the steering bar and sat in front of her.

He hit a switch that extended the wings and cockpit cover as he started the engine, morphing the sky cycle into a two-person flyer for high-speed travel.

They arrived in Chicago about two hours later. New Chicago was smaller than the original. None of the original buildings were salvageable. The first cyborgs that returned to Earth spent months leveling tattered buildings and clearing the land so they could rebuild. Before they could do that, they had to evacuate the people living in the ruins.

Stalker had landed at the shuttle port from the ship that had brought them from Phantom, the cyborg planet. After meeting with Commander Dark, he'd taken off for California on his newly refurbished sky cycle. While en route, he checked the AI net for where they could get Neely outfitted.

True to her word, she only chose a few pairs of black cargo pants and khaki green t-shirts, socks, and a black jacket like those the cyborgs wore. Stalker would have gotten her anything she wanted, but somehow, he knew that would not impress her. She was an independent woman, used to taking care of things herself.

Neely didn't want to depend on him or any other male to get the things she needed or protect her. He didn't delude himself into believing she accepted his offer because she wanted to be with him. She was clearly attracted to him, but she took his deal because it gave her a way out of her dilemma. She only balked when he took her to be measured for body armor like the cyborgs used.

"Why do I need that?" she asked.

"Because where we're going is dangerous. The cities are like a warzone. I've spent most of my time checking on the rural communities so far. They started shooting within minutes of my arrival in Los Angeles."

"You are only one man. Granted, you're a cyborg, but how are you going to fight that all by yourself?"

"Do you know how to use a gun?"

CLARISSA LAKE · CHRISTINE MYERS

"I'm pretty good with a blaster, but mine blew up with my flyer."

"I have weapons. How about an ion rifle?"

"Not my first choice in close quarters. So, I don't have much experience with them. I can fire one, but I didn't hit the target often enough to be useful."

"What about a physical fight?"

"Good enough to get me out of a few jams and some rape attempts."

"This job is dangerous, and I want to make sure you are prepared," he told her.

"I lived in Farringay most of my life, and I've had a few run-ins with gangers. I killed one once."

Neely had a defiant look that almost dared Stalker to ask what happened. He had a pretty good idea.

"Can you read and write?" he asked instead

"My mom taught me when I was a kid. She had some old books handed down through her family that she kept stashed. It would be hard to fly without it."

"And how did you learn to fly? There aren't that many working flyers in this territory."

"My father. He worked for Overlord Berke smuggling. He would come by from time to time and take us up. He started letting me fly it and eventually taught me everything. After he died, I took over."

"What about your mother? Is she still alive?"

"She is. She is a hostess in one of Berke's pleasure houses. She worked her way up from sex worker. I became a sex worker when I got old enough. My father was one of her customers, but he always had a soft spot for Mama and me. He didn't want that life for me, so he taught me to fly.

"One day when he arrived, he was ill. He'd been stabbed in a fight. The wound wasn't life-threatening, but he went septic and died of an infection. Before he died, he told me the flyer was mine."

"That's why you were so upset by its destruction. It was a gift from your dying father."

"Yes."

"But it brought you to me…" he smiled at her. "Let's go get some lunch. We still have a long trip ahead of us. Your armor belt should be ready by the time we come back."

Chapter Five

Gone were the days of world-famous restaurant chains. Stalker took Neely to a diner near the shuttle port, where they had a meal of steak and potatoes.

"How did you get the name Stalker?" Neely asked between bites.

"I chose my name because we stalked the enemy and killed them. I picked Knight because we were defenders of the Federation."

Neely saw something flicker in his eyes that took him back to the war and a very dark place.

"How did you do that year after year? Weren't the cyborg marines in the thick of the fighting on every planet."

"Two things. They programmed our bodies to secrete endorphins when we were in the thick of it. The more enemies we killed, the bigger the risk, the better we liked it."

"That's twisted." Neely frowned.

"When that didn't work, our internal computer would remind us that we would return to Earth to be matched with our genetic mates. The female who would love us, and we would love. We would make children and raise them together. We lived it in virtual reality."

Neely didn't know what to say as she looked into his eyes. He was talking about *her*. Stalker and the other cyborgs had battled year after year for nearly one hundred years for the promise of love. *Her love.*

Could she love him? She thought he deserved to have someone love him. The only thought she had about babies was to get an implant to prevent it. That still had a few years on it.

Stalker was so damned attractive and sexy. Just thinking about running her hands all over those muscles and having them pressed against her made her core throb. That bulge in his pants promised a cock that could fill her amply.

The way he looked at her like she was the girl of his dreams…. Because she was. The guy had been brainwashed with the promise of his perfect mate he could recognize by her pheromones.

Neely felt torn. If she went to California with him, there would be no turning back. It was all or nothing. She had to walk away now or take a leap of faith.

"You're still thinking about it. My fate is in your hands."

"It's not like I can instantly fall in love with you because you say we're genetic mates even if you are sexy as hell and smell good."

Stalker grinned. "That's a start. We can take it one day at a time."

"Just so you know, I have a contraceptive implant. It's got a few years left on it," she said. "I'm not even sure I want to have kids."

"But you aren't sure you don't," he pointed out. "We don't need to have that discussion now."

"Do you really want someone like me to be the mother of your kids? I spent five years as a whore in a brothel before becoming a smuggler…."

"You survived, Neely. Females who lived in the Farringay ruins risked rape and even murder every time they went out to find food."

"That was why my mom went to work for Berke, mainly for food, shelter, and protection. I was an accident, born before she went to work there. Her relationship with my father was complicated. She told me from the start; that he was my father, and he accepted me. Sometimes, he was gone for days and sometimes for months. He was pissed when he returned from one of his months-long excursions to learn I was working at the brothel. That's when he started teaching me to fly and defend myself."

"But you still worked in the brothel for five years…."

"Because Dad was gone a lot, and we didn't have enough money to buy another plane."

"What kind of fighting did he teach you?" Stalker asked.

"Street fighting, stabbing, shooting. …only to fight if I didn't have a choice ….to be aware of my surroundings and look for things that could be used as a weapon. Once I got my blaster, I used that when I needed it."

"I can definitely work with that." Stalker smiled at her. "Beautiful and dangerous."

Neely couldn't help blushing, more at the way he looked at her than what he said. Nothing she had told him changed how he seemed to caress her with his eyes.

"What's the situation in California? I've been up and down the East coast, but I haven't been west."

"Like Farringay but ten times bigger. I've already put in a request for a hundred additional cyborgs. Before the Mesaarkans bombed it, forty million people lived in the city and greater Los Angeles area. Even though the population was decimated, maybe a million people now live in the city ruins."

"Where do we even start?" Neely asked.

"Finish your lunch, and we'll head out."

"You know what I mean."

He smiled at her. "With the villages, we go in and find out who is in charge and see how they run their communities. If they are governed by consensus, we offer them support services from the Enclave to help them restore infrastructure and tech to restore communications."

"Even Farringay is divided into factions. Your Los Angeles is going to have even more divisions and rivalry."

"Seven so far. I explored the city the first month walking, doing recon. My hovercycle would have drawn too much attention since only a few working means of transport are available. Most everyone else is using horses or mules."

"People outside Starport City in Farringay use horses. I never rode one, though."

"Nor have I, but it might be useful to learn," said Stalker.

"Do you live in Los Angeles?" she wondered, taking the last bite of her meal.

"No, I chose a mountain hideaway removed from the city. I wanted a place where my family would be safe, provided I found my genetic mate," he said.

"I like the sound of that—the location."

Stalker noted her qualification but didn't remark on it. She needed more time to get used to the idea that she was his mate. He'd had nearly a hundred years to think about it. Neely had had only a day.

"Now that you have finished eating, we should go," he said, pushing his chair out.

"Yes, I just need to stop at the lavatory beforehand since it will be a long trip."

"That is a good idea. Conditions west are primitive. I will meet you by the exit."

They were in the air ten minutes later, headed west with the sky cycle in flyer mode.

An hour into the flight, so close to Stalker, it was hard to avoid touching him or rubbing her front against his back. Neely knew she was in trouble with her plan to keep him at a distance. He had done nothing since kissing her to push her into accepting his claim. His pheromones were doing it all for him, keeping her in a state of arousal that was hard to fight.

If it was this difficult for her, it must be as bad for him. Going to work with him seemed like a good solution to her problem. Yet, if she gave into the incredible attraction to him, she was in for life. Even if she didn't, Neely doubted she could walk away.

Until Stalker appeared in her life and claimed she was his genetic mate, she hadn't given much thought to a husband or children. She resigned herself to life without a mate because she thought men were shallow and saw women as a place to put their cocks.

Her father was the exception. He was the only man who simply loved her because she was his child.

It seemed utterly surreal that this gorgeous cyborg exploded into her life a day and a half ago.

As the trip wore on, Neely found herself sitting on her hands to keep from running them over Stalker's incredible male body. Every breath she took filled her nostrils with his woodsy scent. She didn't want him to know how he tempted her, although he probably knew.

And he probably knew; all he had to do was bide his time. She wasn't even thinking about love; she wanted him to lay her down and pound his cock into her until she came so hard, she could only scream his name.

Even as she thought it, she knew once would never be enough.

As Stalker flew the sky cycle west, he replayed everything that happened since he pulled Neely from her burning flyer. The odds of his genetic mate dropping out of the sky so close to him were hard to calculate even for him because there was no complete census of the current Earth population. Even estimating the current population, the odds were a fraction of one percent.

The aliens who convinced the Mesaarkans to end the war believed in the power of thought to manifest one's own destiny. Of course, they were powerful psions, possibly the most powerful beings in the galaxy.

Stalker was just a genetically engineered and cybernetically enhanced human.

Could his mind be powerful enough to devise conditions that his destiny would connect with Neely's? After the war, while trying to figure out what he wanted to do next, he had input all the information he could find on the Wholaskans.

He refused to give up on finding his genetic mate after he learned that the Federation never made a plan to find the genetic mates for the cyborgs. While studying the Wholaskans' philosophy of thought, he learned to meditate on his yearning to find his mate.

Two years later, he got the call to return to Earth.

Chapter Six

Neely hadn't talked much after the first hour of their flight to California. Stalker suspected she was still struggling with the potent attraction between them. Scenting her arousal had kept him hard most of the trip. Not until he'd settled the sky cycle in his garage did he realize she had fallen asleep.

Stalker swung his leg over the front of the bike and turned to help Neely off. She sat limply on the passenger seat with her head back against the rest.

"Neely?" He reached up and patted her cheek lightly. "Neely, we are home."

"Tired, so tired," she murmured, not opening her eyes.

She moved as if to turn over in bed, and Stalker caught her arm before she fell onto the concrete floor. He decided not to bother trying to wake her, lifting her into his arms and carrying her into the house. It had been more than thirty hours since he rescued Neely.

Stalker had been active for almost forty hours. During the war, they were often on duty for more than a week at a time without sleep. Their nanites compensated to keep them lucid. The single bolus he'd given her was insufficient to offset the lack of sleep and fix her injuries.

He carried her into his bedroom and laid her on his bed. Briefly considering one of the other two bedrooms, he wanted her close to make sure she merely needed sleep and didn't need further medical intervention. Just to be certain, he scanned her body with his internal computer while he removed her boots.

Covering her with a blanket from the end of the bed, Stalker paused to watch her sleep. Although he keenly anticipated their first mating, he wouldn't rush her into it. He had tamped down his own desire by a supreme effort of will, reminding himself that the avatar he loved all his life only represented his genetic mate.

As a sex worker, he speculated she probably didn't have a choice whether she wanted to have sex or not. He wasn't jealous or disgusted by her past. It was part of her, like the years he had spent at war killing sentient beings and the times he'd been injured and repaired.

Like his friend Darken, he'd been left for dead, but only for hours instead of days. Commander Savage had insisted on coming back for him and carried him out. His commander wasn't leaving without proof.

Along with many cyborgs who fought the war, Stalker had received extensive mental health therapies to deal with the many traumas and PTSD they suffered during and after the war. It didn't wipe their memories, but it distanced them so that it might have happened in another life.

This was a new fight, protecting innocents from those who would prey on them.

Stalker stood beside the bed for a long time, watching Neely sleep, savoring finding her. Of course, she was beautiful to him with her tousled red hair and brown roots. The red was obviously a choice. Though closed in sleep, he remembered the sparks in her blue eyes, not midnight blue like his own, but cool light blue. He empathized with her at the loss of her flyer while glad its loss made it easier to convince her to come west with him.

Stalker would get her another in time… after he was sure she wouldn't use it to leave him. That she wanted him kept him hopeful. Just thinking about breeding with her made him hard again.

He pinged the house AI to lock the doors on his way to the shower. Quickly stripping, he stepped into the alcove, and slid the door closed behind him. Turning on the water spray, he took a bar of handmade soap, rubbing it back and forth on his hand for lubrication.

Fisting his hand around his cock, he stroked up and down its length, remembering how she responded to his kiss. He imagined them both naked as he held her chest to chest, plundering her mouth with his tongue.

He visualized Neely in the shower with him, and he squeezed his cock harder and stroked it faster. With her arms and legs around him, he would grip the rounded cheeks of her ass to shift her so he could slide his cock into her slick opening. He could almost feel her wet heat close around him as he filled her to the hilt.

He'd press her against the wall teasing her nipples, slowly moving in and out of her. Their mouths would be fused together in one long tongue-stroking kiss. As he drove his cock in and out of her, faster and harder, he'd cup her ass and hold her so she wouldn't be slammed against the stone tile wall as he pounded into her.

He stroked harder and faster, chasing the climax he could feel building in his lower spine. She might come first, contracting around him, sending him over the edge of bliss.

Stalker groaned, closing his eyes as he came, shooting his semen onto the floor to be washed down the drain. Eyes still closed, he breathed as he finished milking himself.

With his lust temporarily sated, he finished his shower quickly and shoved his clothes into the cleaner. Padding out to the bedroom naked, he set his boots by the bed and then pulled a pair of boxers from a drawer built into the wall.

After putting them on, he checked to see that Neely was still covered. He turned back the sheet on his side of the bed and slid between them. With Neely safe beside him, it didn't take long for him to fall asleep. It had been a long two days.

Stalker woke immediately when Neely stirred and sat up. She looked around the room, then turned and saw him lying in bed beside her.

"Did you sleep well?" He sat up and leaned back against the bed's head. He slipped from under the cover, revealing the boxers he wore to bed.

"I think so. I don't even remember getting here."

"I tried to wake you, and you almost fell off the bike, so I caught you and carried you in…."

"Thank you." She paused for a moment and frowned. "So, you brought me to your bed?"

"And took off your boots. I wanted you close, and I knew you would be disoriented when you woke up."

"I was until I saw you."

"I had a shower after I put you in bed. The bathroom is in through that door. I brought your clothes in and set them on that table." He pointed. "The shower works on voice commands or by the manual faucets. All I have is bar soap, but the shampoo is in with your clothes."

"I can't believe you bought that. It was so expensive."

"That's because it came from offworld."

"I usually just used the bar soap."

He shrugged. "I can afford it. I still have most of the pay from the war. Most of us do. During the war, everything was provided… And we thought we would get our mates after it ended. We saved our credits for taking care of our mates and family."

CLARISSA LAKE · CHRISTINE MYERS

"But you're going to give me time to think about this mating thing." It was more a statement than a question."

"Yes, Neely." His tone was gentle, and he reached for her hand and brought it to his lips. "You will tell me when you wish to breed."

"I think you know I want you."

"And I know you are not ready." He rubbed his thumb back and forth over the back of her hand. "I'm going to get dressed, and we will have breakfast when you're showered and dressed. I have a food processor with an extensive menu."

Neely realized she was disappointed that Stalker didn't even kiss her. Remembering their first kiss, she knew it wouldn't take much more than that for her to forget her reluctance and give him what they both wanted. The lifetime commitment stopped her from asking to 'breed' with him.

She wished she could talk to another woman who had a cyborg husband, but she didn't know any. Picking up the duffel containing her new clothes, she picked an outfit and carried it into the bathroom.

A cold shower might cool her libido, but she hated being cold. Besides, it would resurge as soon as she got near Stalker again.

She thought about taking matters into her own hands to get an orgasm, but that would only last until she got near him again.

Neely hung her clothes on a hook and used the faucets to turn on the shower. She stepped under it and started shampooing her hair. After rinsing her hair, she soaped up a cloth to wash her body. Even though she finished bathing quickly, she stood under the shower for a long time afterward, just thinking, basking in the luxury of warm water running over her body.

Would it be so bad to spend her life with a gorgeous, sexy man like Stalker? Was he really as nice as he seemed? And guileless? He was giving her time to figure it out, and she could barely think of anything else.

For Stalker, it was settled. She was his genetic mate. That was all he needed to know to accept her as his lifemate without knowing anything about her. He came preconditioned to love her. Could he possibly be that perfect?

Chapter Seven

Finding the kitchen was easy when Neely had finished her shower and dressed. The bedroom opened to a short hallway to the living room, which flowed into it. Stalker was setting steamy mugs on the breakfast nook's table for two, along with two plates of scrambled eggs and toast.

"The shower was wonderful." Neely smiled as he gestured for her to take the seat across from where he was about to sit.

"You don't have to worry about how much water you use. We don't have a shortage, and we recycle it."

"Good to know. Is that coffee?"

"Yes. Is that okay? Do you want something else?" He started to get up.

"No, I want coffee. With a bit of sugar if you have it. Or I can drink it black."

"I have sugar." Stalker reached up on the counter that divided the dining area from the food processing region and retrieved a small canister with an opening in the top.

She took it and poured some on a spoon, stirred it into her coffee, and handed it back to him. Sticking a fingertip into the hot coffee, she jerked it back out. Too hot, so she picked up her fork and started eating the eggs on her plate.

"What do you plan for today?"

"I want to teach you how to activate your armor and set you up with some weapons so I can test your ability before we go out in the field."

"Every time I go into the city, somebody shoots at me. So far, it's been projectile weapons. This new armor will protect even from armor-piercing projectiles. Blasters can still stun you, but ion rifles could hurt you."

Neely listened intently, watching his lips move as he spoke, remembering how they felt against hers when he kissed her. Then she mentally shook herself.

"It sure sounds like Farringay. I had a couple harrowing experiences the two times I ventured outside Starport city."

"What did you do?"

"I ran. Hid and ran the other way after they ran past me. Another time two guys grabbed me, but Berke's bodyguard ran them off."

"From now on, I will protect you. I won't hesitate to kill anyone who tries to hurt you," Stalker vowed.

Neely didn't doubt him, seeing the intensity in his eyes. He was all hot alpha male ready to take on any foe who threatened his mate. She could easily imagine he would bring that passion to their mating. It was a real turn-on that made her core clench.

"I would do the same for you," she asserted, frowning as she realized what she said. She was fooling herself if she thought she could walk away from this man. Yet she still couldn't let herself go all in.

"I believe you," Stalker responded with a slight smile. "But I don't want you putting yourself in danger for me. Even with armor, you are still more vulnerable than I am without it."

Neely nodded and scooped another fork full of eggs into her mouth. She needed to distract herself from her attraction to him. She didn't speak again until she had finished eating. "I will need that com-tablet you promised me. I need to let my mom know I am all right, and tell Berke what happened… and get in touch with some… Other people."

"Sure, you can use the communications room. Come with me." He stood, and she followed suit.

As she stood, she glanced around the living room. *This is a really nice house.*

The communications room was through a door off the living room that opened automatically when Stalker approached. There was a box on the shelf that contained the house AI system. A floor-to-ceiling door on the right slid open revealing shelf after shelf of brand-new com-tablets. He took one off the top shelf and handed it to Neely.

"It's already synced with our communication satellites, so you can start using it immediately," he said. "You can sit at the desk here, and I will let you have privacy to make your calls."

The desk was shiny and black, apparently molded in one piece. The padded chair was cast from the same material with a roller system hidden under its base.

"It's okay; I'm just calling Mom right now."

"If you don't mind, I will bring up the holographic map to see where we can start tomorrow."

71

"That's fine," Neely said and touched the screen to bring up the menu. "Call Vanessa Albert in Farringay." After pinging the requested code several times, Neeley's mother appeared on the small screen.

"Omigod, Neely! Where have you been? It's been three days."

"Argh! You would not believe it, Mom. One of White's damn cyborgs shot down my flyer for no reason. A nice cyborg ranger pulled me out before it exploded and burned. I don't know what the fuck he was thinking."

"A cyborg rescued you?" Vanessa questioned with interest.

"Yes, his name is Stalker Knight, and he says I am his genetic mate. I know it sounds crazy…."

"No. No, it's not. You remember, Mr. Berke discovered he had a daughter?"

"What about it?"

"She married a cyborg, her genetic mate. He's gorgeous, and Mr. Berke says his daughter adores him. Berke really doesn't like the Enclave cyborgs, but he tolerates this one because he treats his daughter so well."

"Good to know. He's right here. Would you like to meet him?"

"Of course." Her mother smiled.

Neely stood and turned to Stalker. "Here, Stalker Knight, meet my mother, Vanessa Albert."

"Well, Mr. Knight, aren't you handsome."

"Thank you, ma'am; you can call me Stalker."

"And thank you, Stalker, for saving Neeley. She's the only family I have. Neely, did you at least deliver the weapons?"

Stalker went back to studying his map.

"I couldn't. They started shooting when I was approaching to land, so I left at full throttle, and two flyers chased me. The cyborgs shot them down, but Colton hit my engine before that. The weapons were all destroyed with my flyer. I haven't told Mr. Berke yet. You are my first call. My old com-unit was destroyed in the flyer."

"Honey, that's not on you when White's henchman shot down the flyer carrying the weapons," said Vanessa. "Do you want me to tell him what happened?"

"No!" Neely was adamant. "I'll tell him. I doubt he will send someone after me for ten rifles."

"Then he will deal with me," Stalker growled behind her.

"I'm sure it will be okay," Vanessa assured her. "Mr. Berke is a reasonable man."

Neely laughed. "If you say so."

"At least tell me where you are."

"Don't," Stalker murmured. "She is safe with me." Stalker said the last loud enough for Vanessa to hear.

"That's not a good idea, Mom… Just in case Mr. Berke isn't as reasonable as you think. I knew you would be worried. I'll call again soon." They ended the call with 'love-you,' and Neely cut the feed.

She made her next call to Berke, who sounded pretty pissed that he was out a hundred thousand credits for the weapons. "Then you should have a chat with Devlin White. His cyborg enforcer Colton Price shot my flyer and made me crash. I barely got out before it exploded and destroyed the merchandise."

"Now, why would I believe that? White was expecting the delivery."

"You can believe her, Mr. Berke. I saw her get shot down and pulled her out before it blew up and burned. Price claimed she was not who he was looking for."

"Who the fuck are you?"

"Federation Cyborg Ranger Stalker Knight. Neely is my female. I think you know what that means."

"Yeah, you're one of those vat boys who can't lie."

"Then we understand each other."

"We're done," said Neely ending the transmission.

Then she looked up at Stalker and frowned, unable to decide whether to chastise him for butting in or thank him.

"I've been taking care of myself for quite a few years now." She looked at him pointedly.

"I didn't like the way he was talking to you." Stalker cupped his hand against her cheek. "You nearly died. You would be dead if I'd been ten seconds slower... That would have broken me ...to find you and lose you in the same moment."

Chapter Eight

Neely could hardly breathe as she looked up at him. The flash of terror in his eyes as he said it left no doubt in her mind just what she meant to him. He needed her. No way could she turn away from this man who spent his whole life fighting a war to finally have someone to love.

She set her com-tablet on the desk and stood, stepping closer to him, sliding her arms around him in a hug as she rested her cheek against his chest. As fierce and deadly as she knew he must be, Stalker was also vulnerable.

He hesitated for a second before he wrapped her in his arms and kissed the top of her head.

Neely wasn't thinking in terms of her feelings. Stalker saved her life before he ever knew she was his genetic mate. If anyone deserved to feel loved, he did.

He felt good pressed against her body, and she wasn't surprised to feel his growing erection against her belly.

Neely liked him, and she wanted him. That was as good a reason as any to fuck him. It had been a long time since she had fucked anyone and even longer since she had wanted to. Aside from her desire, she wanted to make Stalker feel loved.

Stalker seemed more than willing to just hold her, despite how his body reacted to her. True to his word, he left it to Neely to determine how far things should go.

She leaned back and looked up at him, running her hands up over his chest and around his neck.

"It's kind of nice to have a man around who cares enough to protect me." She smiled. "Especially one I am so attracted to… Stalker… I want to breed with you. We've got chemistry like I have never felt before…

Stalker looked down at her, a little stunned that she had said exactly what he wanted to hear. "Yes, I will breed with you." He whispered and lowered his head to claim her lips in a passionate kiss.

As he deepened the kiss, he gripped her buttocks and lifted her so she could wrap her legs around him. Their tongues tangoed around, rubbing together and exploring. Pleasurable sensations rippled through her body, drawing her nipples into hard peaks and making her clit throb…

Neely kissed him back, squeezing her breasts against his chest and caressing his head and neck. He groaned softly as she rubbed her body against him throughout the kiss.

Stalker finally broke the kiss, nuzzling her neck as he carried Neely to the bedroom. She hugged him and laid her head on his shoulder. He pinged the door to close behind them and crossed the floor to the bed.

Neely raised her head to look into his eyes, and he seemed a bit awed. He had dreamed of this moment all his life, finally claiming his female by pouring his seed inside her.

She smiled tenderly at him and stroked his cheek with the back of her fingers. Then she held his face between her hands and teased him with butterfly kisses for seconds before he pressed his mouth to hers in a dominating kiss.

She opened readily for him sighing her surrender. He loved the way she caressed him as he plundered her mouth. Sliding his hands under her shirt, he flicked her erect nipples with his thumbs. Neely made soft whimpering sounds in her throat and ground her pussy against his belly.

Stalker soon ended the kiss and pushed her legs down, urging her to stand in front of him. Pulling his shirt off over his head, he dropped it to the floor and waited for Neely to remove hers, toeing off his boots.

She crossed her arms, gripping the hem, and pulled it off over her head, leaving her bare from the waist up. Her shirt had a smart fabric insert that supported her breasts, so no bra was necessary.

They felt heavy and sensitive as she perused his taut six-pack, pecks, and broad shoulders. When her eyes reached his, she smiled and pulled open the hook-loop closure on her pants. Pushing them to the floor, she stood and stepped out of them, naked.

Stalker didn't make a move, though she could see the raw desire in his eyes. Neely understood he would not take what was not freely given at that moment.

She moved closer, gripped his pants waist, and pulled open the hook-loop closure, freeing his engorged cock. It was large and exquisitely shaped with a drop of precum at the tip. Pausing to lick it off, she pushed his trousers to the floor.

Stalker stepped out of them, and she pushed them away, smiling up at him. Taking one knee, she caressed his cock from hilt to tip, then enjoyed the silky texture with her lips and cheeks. She was rewarded with his sudden intake of breath.

He was so wonderfully male; she wanted to worship every inch of his body. Teasing him a little, she dragged her tongue over his shaft to the hilt then kissed her way up his body, using her hands to stroke his cock on the way up.

Groaning his pleasure, he ran his fingers through her short hair and explored her shoulders and back. Neely purred and rubbed her taut nipples against his body as she kissed her way up.

Standing on her toes, she leaned against him, putting her arms around his neck, and urged him to bow his head for a passionate kiss.

Stalker lifted her up and urged her to wrap her legs around him as he delved inside her mouth with his tongue. Neely's clit throbbed, and her inner walls clenched. She moaned softly and ground her wet pussy against his belly.

He knelt on the bed, maneuvered them to the middle, and lowered her onto the bed beneath him.

"Stalker, I want you so much. Please, fuck me now," she whispered urgently when he freed her mouth.

"Say you're mine!" he demanded in an urgent whisper.

"I am yours." Neely had already decided before she asked him to breed. She wasn't in love with him, but she believed it would happen. She wasn't just thinking with her pussy, either. It was logical to accept Stalker as her mate because they were genetically matched.

"And I am yours," he repeated.

Neely uncrossed her ankles and moved her feet flat on the bed spreading her legs wide to give him access. Raising her hips, she rubbed against the length of his cock.

Stalker accepted the invitation and put the tip of his cock at her entrance. He was a big male with a larger than average cock, so she was a tight fit. It had been that long since she'd had sex.

81

He pulled back and thrust a little further in, letting her juices lubricate him. A few more times, and he was all the way inside her.

"Ah, you feel wonderful," she murmured with a sigh, hugging his cock inside her.

"Yes, I do." Stalker kissed her and slid his hands between them to pinch and roll her nipples between his fingers. Holding his weight on his elbows, he stared into Neely's eyes.

Gazing back at him tenderly, she stroked his cheek with the backs of her fingers, then caressed him wherever she could reach. How could she not have tender feelings for this enhanced male who looked at her as though she meant everything to him?

Neely loved the feeling of his big body pressing down on hers and how his cock filled her.

He thrust in and out of her as though savoring every one. Turning his gaze to her soft parted lips, Stalker kissed her again, dominating her mouth with his tongue stroking and twirling around hers. As she responded, he started thrusting faster and harder, his hard chest pressing down on her breasts and rubbing against her sensitive nipples each time.

Fucking him was utter bliss as he stroked her G-spot each time he plunged into her. His rhythm increased faster and faster until he was pounding into her. Neely tilted her pelvis upward, meeting him thrust for thrust, and soon she could feel her orgasm building.

Her muscles tightened until it took her into her first climax, squeezing his cock while he continued to pound into her. Neely moaned into his mouth as her body jerked beneath him, and she dug her short fingernails into his back.

She knew he couldn't stop to tease her through it, so she rode it out in complete surrender. Yet she never felt so free. She chose to accept her attraction to him. Stalker's only advance had been a single kiss.

Neely had never experienced spontaneous sexual attraction to a man before. Being Stalker's genetic match seemed to explain it. She came twice while he pounded into her, then again when he came, spilling hot nanite laden semen into her womb.

Stalker shouted inarticulately at the intensity of it. Neely cried out his name as her climax racked her body again. His thrusting slowed, going deep, and he groaned each time her inner walls squeezed around his cock.

They rode the waves of pleasure that ebbed and flowed until their orgasm played out.

Stalker collapsed against her, still inside her, and she hugged him tightly, taking shallow breaths as he pressed her into the bed. Seconds later, he raised his weight on his forearms and kissed her lips tenderly.

"You are mine!" he whispered. "As long as I draw breath…."

"And you are mine as long as I draw breath," she agreed. *I sure hope you are right, Mom. No way is this gorgeous cyborg ever letting me go. And I hope I don't ever want him to.*

Chapter Nine

Stalker rolled them over, so she was on top of him, still joined. Neely couldn't help smiling at him simply because he was smiling up at her.

"You were fantastic!" they both said at the same time.

Neely giggled and dropped a light kiss on his lips. No frills sex had never felt so good. Mainly, they had been so horny for each other almost since they met.

Considering Stalker had waited his whole life to find and claim his genetic mate, she was pretty sure they were not finished yet. He was still hard inside her. Apparently, this super soldier also possessed enhanced sexual prowess as well.

"You are so beautiful," he said, caressing her back and buttocks.

Neely held his face between her hands and stroked his cheeks with her thumbs.

"You make me feel beautiful when you look at me like that. …And you are just as beautiful with your gorgeous midnight eyes and all your muscles. …. Not to mention that impressive cock that feels so good inside me."

She gave him a slow, tender kiss.

Stalker rolled them over again, taking back the dominant position. "Since you like it so well, would you like some more?" he asked hopefully, his lips barely parted from hers.

"Yes, please," she murmured, squeezing his cock inside her.

Before the sun set, they had sex three more times, once in the shower as Stalker had fantasized when he'd pleasured himself there. That round had been far more satisfying than he'd imagined.

After the last time, Stalker could see that Neely was exhausted. He carried her into the bathroom, helped her get cleaned up, and put her back into bed. While she dozed, he went to the kitchen and brought sandwiches and juice for them both. They ate them sitting in bed; Stalker took the plates and tumblers to the washer in the kitchen. By the time he came back to the bedroom, Neely had fallen asleep.

Stalker stood there for a long time watching her, letting himself bask in the joy of claiming his mate. He had planned to show her the rest of the house and the yard around it. There was no way he could deny her when she asked him to breed. The constant erection was getting damned uncomfortable, but letting her make that decision was important.

He thought he could probably have seduced her with kisses and caresses, using her attraction and arousal to turn her on so much that she would give in to her desire. Only afterward, she might regret it and not consent to be his mate.

Stalker doubted she was in love with him. He'd heard her mother tell her to accept him because he was conditioned to love her and take care of her. Cyborgs were good mates.

Neely responded mostly to pheromones that made her want to breed with him. Yet, it was more than that. When they coupled, he could feel she was all into it and not just doing it to please him. Her caring seemed real as if she had a gut feeling that being with him was right for her.

Nothing had felt so right to him. He almost wished he didn't have California to pull back into the fold. The Los Angeles megalopolis had eaten up the greater L.A. areas, including some towns. So many people died, and their skeletons remained in the ruins.

Stalker understood why Vyken Dark started the restoration at Chicago. It was the home of the Civil Restoration Enclave, an organization formed decades before the war to restore civilization to North America after an apocalyptic event.

Their scientists were responsible for developing cybernetic technology and combining it with genetically engineered humans to defend and reclaim the Earth. Many cyborgs didn't want to return to Earth when the war was finally over. They were so broken that even the promise of their genetic mates was not enough to pull them back.

They had started the cyborg colony on Phantom. It was a place where they could heal for as long as it took for recovery. Some cyborgs never left, but Stalker's marine ranger team took the rehab treatment and psychotherapy, so they could come back and find their mates.

Learning there was no plan to find the promised mates was a big setback for many cyborgs. Stalker's team was angry and disheartened. Then Commander Savage reminded them of how many times they'd done the impossible during the war. Earth was where they were most likely to find their mates.

Vyken Dark's invitation to help tame the western states was the incentive they needed to go back. What's more, they'd built a genetic database of females wanting cyborg mates.

Now that Stalker had found Neely, three of their six-man team had mates. He planned to encourage friends still on Phantom to come to Earth. After all they'd been through, he wanted them to know the joy of finding their genetic mates.

He could still remember it all, but it no longer caused him emotional pain as it had the months after the war when his psyche was still in combat mode. Now his job was restorative… To protect the innocent from those who would use and abuse them.

He couldn't suppress a tender smile as he watched Neely sleep. He couldn't stop looping their breeding, the way she touched him and clung to him while he pounded into her. She seemed to revel in their coupling and held him tenderly when he was spent from their powerful orgasm.

Finally, Stalker slid into bed behind her as she slept on her side and cuddled against her spoon fashion.

Neely woke after a full night's sleep to find Stalker laying on his side with his head propped against his hand, watching her. He smiled and stroked her cheek with his fingertip when she looked at him.

"Morning," she said. He seemed so happy; she was glad she decided to go ahead and fuck him. Admittedly she had done it as much to satisfy her own desires as to quell his.

Living without sex for so long, she was practically a born-again virgin. Neely expected to be sore down there after so much sex, but she wasn't. All those nanites he pumped in with his semen must have taken that away.

Stalker wasn't just a big guy; he had a big cock, too. It had been a tight fit.

As Stalker's gaze heated, she didn't have to be a mind reader to know what he was thinking. It was enough to make her pussy clench. Just that look had set her whole body on alert. And they were still naked from last night.

Neely sat up and turned back the covers, excusing herself to use the bathroom.

She knew it had to be that pheromone thing, at least partly. Her nipples were taut, and her pussy was practically dripping when she came back and slid into bed beside Stalker.

"I sense your arousal. Do you wish to breed?" he asked casually as if offering a cup of tea.

"Only if you are up for it."

"I will always be up for it with you." He gave her a sexy smirk and leaned over to kiss her.

At first, it was a feathery brush of his lips over hers. Then he drew Neely to the bed's middle and lay over her with a muscular thigh pressed on her mons. His lips settled on hers in a slow sensual kiss. Sliding his tongue into her mouth, he swirled it around hers while kneading her breast with his palm.

Neely mewled softly as Stalker plucked her erect nipple, then he moved his leg, running his hand over her belly to cup her mons. Dipping two fingers into her wet slit, he found her g-spot and stroked it a few times, pumping his fingers in and out.

She squirmed as he took her arousal to a new level, moaning against his mouth. She could have taken him right then, but Stalker seemed in no hurry.

Ending the kiss, he pulled his fingers out of her and brought them to his mouth. Pausing to breathe in her musk, he licked them clean with an "Mm."

Next, he pushed her legs apart and rolled over between them. Neely drew her knees up, thinking he would take her, but he started kissing her forehead, eyelids, nose, cheeks, then her lips, dipping his tongue for a thorough exploration.

He moved his mouth to her earlobe to nibble and suck on it. Dragging his lips over her jawline and down her neck, pausing to nip and taste the sensitive spot where her shoulder met her neck.

Her nipples tightened, and her clit clamored for his attention, while Stalker seemed intent on branding every inch of her flesh with his lips and tongue. Neely instinctively tilted her pelvis to rub her clit against his cock, resting lengthwise on her mons.

He took a full tour of her upper chest before his mouth clamped over one nipple. Stalker gently pinched it between his teeth before sucking on it. Waves of pleasure surged to her clit and sent her into a delightful orgasm.

"I will tease you until you scream my name, and then we will breed," he promised, pressing on her clit with his cock, sending a new wave of shudders through her.

That took the edge off until he suckled her other nipple making her squirm and moan as her hands fisted in his short hair. Her climax had played out when he began working his way down her ribcage and belly.

Her clit throbbed as she anticipated what would come next. Only, as he reached her mons and parted the hair over her clit and opening, he blew his warm breath on her engorged bud.

Panting, Neely cried out, clenching her channel. Her whole body quivered with the need to come again, but Stalker wouldn't make it that easy. He planted kisses on her inner thigh, licking and nipping down her leg and up the other. Finally, he reached her core, dragging his tongue up her slit to her clit.

She bucked her hips until Stalker gripped her thighs, holding them apart. Unable to grasp the sheet beneath them, Neely's hands fisted at her sides while she sobbed her approval in drawn-out oh's and ah's. He slipped two fingers inside her, moving them in and out as he flicked her clit with his tongue and sucked it.

She held back as long as she could until she could only scream Stalker's name as he promised she would. He kept lapping at her folds until she pushed him away, too sensitive to take any more.

As hard as she had come, clenching his fingers, she still needed him inside her. Stalker wiped his face, moved back to her side, and pulled her into his arms, just holding her for a time. Neely just closed her eyes and pressed her cheek against his throat savoring his caresses down her back. Sex with Stalker was the best ever.

After a respite, Neely suggested he take her from behind, crouched on her forearms and knees with her ass in the air. She came at least twice more, the second time when he did, and she saw stars behind her eyelids.

Chapter Ten

After a shower, donning fresh clothes, and eating a light breakfast, Stalker finally showed her the rest of the house. It was an elongated domed structure made from lightweight aerated concrete with nodules for two other bedrooms and the master bedroom. Each bedroom had its own bathroom.

The garage was off the kitchen and doubled as a workout space. Two punching bags, a cylindrical and a bulbous air-filled bag hanging from a bar. There were also free weights and a bench, plus floor mats.

The living room, dining area, and kitchen were all contained in one open space. Each section held rustic wooden furniture. The living room couch and chairs were cushioned with extra pillows for additional comfort. The floor was polished concrete with low maintenance area rugs.

Skylights and windows let in natural light during the day with lighted ceiling fixtures for after dark. The house was powered and heated by geothermal energy. With the national grid down for a century, each home needed its own energy source.

"What do you think?" Stalker asked when he finished explaining everything.

"It makes my one-room flat in Starport City look like a closet. And those bedrooms are huge."

"One for girls and one for boys," he said, "with room to partition them off as they get older and require more privacy."

"Just how many children do you think we will have?"

"I was hoping for at least two, but I knew it would be something we would decide together. Until then, we have guest rooms if we ever need them."

"Very diplomatic," she said with a smile, looking up at him. "I am still getting used to the idea that I have a sexy cyborg mate I barely know. There is still a part of me asking myself if I am out of my mind to make that commitment after getting laid once for the first time in about eight years."

"You regret that?" Stalker's brows knit in a troubled frown.

"That's not what I meant. I'm just not that impulsive---especially not about men. Then you came along, Mister Tall, Dark and

Hot, and I am practically begging you to fuck me."

"Because we are genetic mates. Your body recognizes that even before your mind."

"I get that. It's just a little unsettling," she said, taking his hand in both of hers. "You are not like most of the cyborgs I have met. They were made cyborgs because of war injuries. They are not brainwashed to have only one genetic mate."

"Many are not happy about their transformations," Stalker said. "They consider themselves less than human, and they didn't get the therapy we received after the war ended. They chose not to. My kind didn't have a choice."

"But you are not complaining?"

"It was, at times, a painful process as our emotions were no longer suppressed. Their psychotherapy gave us the peace we would not have otherwise."

"I can relate to that, after five years as a sex worker, commonly known as a whore. And you're okay with that?"

"Many females have been forced to trade sex for safety or food to survive. Or they endured rape to avoid being beaten or killed.

CLARISSA LAKE · CHRISTINE MYERS

What you did before was part of the woman you have become, of who you are now, my mate."

Neely nodded, not knowing what to say.

"My life with you started three days ago when I pulled you out of your burning flyer. Before therapy, I lived to kill beings, sentient beings determined to destroy our species."

"They made a pretty good start when they bombed Earth. There are cities back East that have been abandoned and whole towns empty with their buildings untouched but deteriorated from neglect."

"We've found it's like that worldwide," Stalker said. "It's the same here in California. The communities that managed the best were those with enough self-sufficient people who were prepared and helped their friends and neighbors meet their needs."

"What about neighbors? Do we have any?" Neely asked.

"Not human ones. We are in what was once a national forest. I was granted permission to buy this parcel to build our home for security reasons. I wanted a safe place for my family. Not everyone will welcome us with open arms. Let's go outside so you can see the property."

Stalker kept her hand in his, and they walked out into a meadow surrounded by a forest of conifers. The house was nestled among a small stand of young sequoias. There was no road or even a walking path nearby.

Off to one side, there was a row of objects that Neely couldn't identify. "What are those?" she pointed.

"Targets. They can be stationary, or they can hover and move around."

"Good, I can use the practice."

"And we will practice. We have a practice setting on our weapons that will fire low-level laser beams, and the targets will beep when you hit them and calculate your accuracy rate."

"How about physical fighting? You said you've done that."

"Yeah. My father taught me some, and one of the cyborg converts trained me some in mixed martial arts. I learned enough to get out of a few jams."

"I will teach you more. We will just make our presence known in Los Angeles. From what I've seen so far, it's gangers and overlords like Farringay outside Starport City."

"How are you going to civilize that?" Neely asked as they strolled around the meadow near the tree line. "Some of those guys will shoot you if you look at them wrong."

"Bullets won't penetrate my skin far enough to do much damage, and they won't pierce our armor," he said confidently. "Do you know if the Eastern Overlords do business with these overlords?"

"I only know I've never transported anything this far west."

"Darken Wolf, one of the cyborgs in my marine ranger team, has evidence that Overlord Devlin White is trafficking humans from New Mexico. That's why we were there doing recon."

"That still doesn't explain why Colton Price pursued and shot my flyer down. No way did he mistake my flyer for one of your sky cycles. They are an entirely different configuration." Neely spouted bitterly. "He wouldn't make that mistake."

"He said; you weren't who he was after," Stalker said, reviewing the incident on his internal computer.

"That doesn't make any sense. Price had to know it was my flyer. If he wasn't trying to kill me, why would he shoot down my flyer with me in it?"

Stalker stopped and turned to face her, still holding her hand. "I think it was your cargo. He prevented you from delivering the ion rifles to Overlord White."

"But, he's one of White's henchmen. He's been there for almost a year."

"He could be a Federation plant or an agent of a rival overlord. Whatever his agenda, I don't think he is on White's side," said Stalker.

"He didn't have to blow up my flyer. He could have just intercepted the weapons." Neely pouted.

"I could kill him for you...."

Neely's mouth dropped open, and her eyes went wide as she looked up at him. He was serious!

"Uh, no thanks. I'm upset about my flyer. Besides, you shot down his flyer," she admitted. She paused, looking around. "Stalker, this place is beautiful, and the house blends right in."

The smooth exterior was nearly the same color as grass with a matte finish.

"We also have a holographic cloaking system and shields."

"That's reassuring… But how would anyone even find this place?"

"They would need the coordinates. The AI surveillance system will activate cloaking if anything other than wildlife breaches our perimeter."

"I've never been this deep into a forest before. It would be easy to get lost if I left the property."

"I would find you," Stalker assured her. "Otherwise, take your com-tablet with you. It is synced with the house AI, and it would guide you back. The commlink in your armor would do the same, and it would guide you back to me if we were separated."

"Okay, then… Maybe we should start with the body armor. How soon do you plan for us to go to L.A.?"

"Not for a few days at least. I want to evaluate your skills before I take you out in the field." Stalker turned and started walking back to the house with her hand still in his. "Let's go get out your armor belt so you can see how it works, then try some sparring so I can evaluate your skills."

"In armor?"

"Yes, I don't want to accidentally hurt you. This armor is made from a nanite laced material that assembles on command from your weapons belt. It forms in two layers with a cushion of air sealed between them," he explained as they strolled back across the meadow. "We normally don't wear anything under it, but mine is integrated into my skin."

"But mine comes with an undergarment, they said."

"You may as well be naked. It fits like a second   skin."

Chapter Eleven

A few minutes later, Neely took the undergarment from the plastic case containing her combination weapon's belt and armor storage. It came in two pieces and looked barely big enough to fit a baby. Constructed of smart fabric, the tank top stretched easily as she slipped her hands through the armholes and pulled it on.

She saw Stalker watching with interest as she pulled it down over her breasts. Though very thin, the black material was fully opaque and molded to her breasts, supporting them. However, it didn't hide her nipples as they tightened in response to Stalker's heated gaze.

Not now! She admonished her body as her core fluttered. It didn't help that Stalker was naked to activate his armor. She turned her back to him and pulled on the skin-tight shorts, which were snug but not binding.

Next, she fastened the belt on to ride just above her hipbones. Pressing the button on the front, she waited while a dark gray liquid expanded until her entire body was encased. It felt like a swarm of bugs slithering over her body and made her shiver with the crawling feeling creeping over her.

Once she was encased, there was no other sensation of movement over her skin. She found the armor flexed with movement by doing some stretches, bending, and moving her limbs.

"Wow, this is a lot more comfortable than I expected," she said through the face shield.

"It's better than our earlier armor. We didn't get this until the last few years of the war. Let's go to the garage, and you can show me what you can do."

They went into the gym and faced off on the mat.

"We're going to do this light contact. I don't want to hurt you; I just want to see what moves you have." Stalker took a martial arts pose, and Neely took her favorite stance, waiting for him to make the first move.

He feigned a punch at her face, and Neely ducked, raising her leg to kick him in the chest. Stalker grabbed her ankle. She used his hold as leverage to drive her knee into his abdomen and her ankle against his crotch.

Before she lost balance, she managed to bring her fist to his throat. Although he could have easily stopped her, Stalker wanted to see what she would do. He released her ankle, gripped her waist, and set her on her feet.

105

"Again." Stalker backed off and resumed his start position.

They danced around each other for a minute while Stalker continued throwing punches that Neely dodged or blocked. She mimed a few of her own, then he mimed a hit that would have knocked her on her ass. Neely blocked and might have flipped an ordinary man onto his back, but cyborgs were a hundred pounds heavier than a normal man of the same size who would have outweighed her by close to a hundred pounds.

"That'll do for now," Stalker told her, retracting his tinted faceplate and helmet. "Let's go to the weapons room, and I'll show you what we have available. Then we'll take some out and see how your aim is."

The weapons room was the size of a walk-in closet with an array of rifles, handheld laser-blasters, knives, and even a rocket launcher.

"There." Neely pointed to a combo pistol-type laser-blaster. "That's like the one I had."

"Okay. It's fully charged; let's take it outside to the targets." He handed one to her, took another for himself, and led the way out. "Now that you've had it on for a while, what do you think of your armor.

"It feels great; it's so light and elastic. I can move any way I want without it binding."

"Exactly as it should be."

The targets looked like a row of fat round posts until Stalker activated them. A round screen about a foot in diameter opened on the top, looking almost like a head.

Standing with Stalker about thirty feet from the targets, Neely waited for instructions.

"See how many you can hit," he said.

Neely took out her weapon, set it for simulation, and stood with her feet shoulder-width apart. Holding the gun with both hands, she squeezed off eight shots and hit every one. She looked up at Stalker when she finished, and he was grinning.

"Not bad. Now let's see how you do when they come at you."

"All of them?" Her eyes widened a bit.

"Don't worry; they stop before they run into you if you don't hit them." Stalker stepped off to the side. "Ready?'

"Yes."

The targets moved toward her at random intervals. Neely fired at the closest ones first.

107

When she hit one, it stopped advancing. She hit only half of them for the first round, and she was disappointed.

"Of course, you know you'd probably be dead if they'd been shooting at you."

"Yeah, I figured."

"We're in the open here. Would you stand there and wait for them if shooters came after you?"

"Hell, no! I'd shoot back, run for cover, and try to pick them off from there."

Stalker nodded and signaled them to return to their bases from his internal computer. "Let's try this again."

"Ready."

The targets advanced this time, and Neely shot the two closest and retreated along the front of the house, stopping and hitting three more. Dashing around the end of the house, she came back out and picked off another two. She jumped out seconds later and picked off the last one.

Each target stopped where she'd hit it.

"Nice shots," Stalker said with a pleased look. "Of course, they'd be shooting back if they were real."

"Isn't that what this armor is for?" she asked cheekily, retracting her helmet.

"It is, but the force of the shot could send you flying even if it doesn't penetrate your body. You can still break bones or get a concussion."

"Noted. That makes sense. Now, what?"

"We're done for now. I'm still in the process of adapting to this new job. Our rangers' team was combat specialists used to being in the thick of the fighting. I had virtual retraining before we even left Phantom, but there are a lot of variables that have affected the social structure of these communities."

"So, we won't know what we are getting into until we get there?"

"That's right. There are so many different factions. They are not communities in the same sense as the more isolated towns outside the city. It's chaotic in L.A., and they seem to be ruling by thuggery rather than consensus." Stalker explained.

"I think you may need way more than a hundred additional protectors for L.A."

A week later, Stalker tooled the sky cycle along an eastern Los Angeles suburb's crumbled, rubble-strewn street. He'd previously scouted the area and headed for an abandoned building to stash the hovercycle.

Pulling the bike into the building, they both climbed off. Stalker and Neely put on their weapons belts and their body armor. They each took out their ion rifles and shouldered them. Before they left the tattered building, Stalker set the cloaking field on the cycle.

Stalker set a moderate pace as they headed into Sector Six. He'd divided the city into ten sectors from previous reconnaissance that were spaced far enough apart to suggest they should be rebuilt as separate towns. He'd submitted his recommendations to the Enclave when he requested a hundred cyborgs to assist him.

"I chose Sector Six because it has a small population. That doesn't mean that no one will shoot at us, so we wear the full helmet and faceplate."

It was a five-minute walk from where they had stashed the sky cycle to the area where Stalker had scanned some people among the ruins. He and Neely walked slowly, looking around for movement.

110

Then Stalker's internal scanner alerted him to people behind him. He stopped, shrugged his rifle strap off his shoulder, turned, and aimed it toward six males pointing an assortment of guns at them.

"Who are you, and what do you want?" said a tall, dark-haired bearded man.

"I am Federation Ranger Stalker Knight. The war is over. We have returned to Earth to help restore civilization." He lowered his rifle as he spoke. Neely remained facing the opposite direction to watch his back, pistol drawn.

Sure enough, four more males with guns stepped out of the ruins behind them.

"Central government has been restored in New Chicago, under the Civil Restoration Enclave of North America. I am the law enforcer in charge of this territory."

"What if we don't want no law enforcer telling us what to do?" said the leader.

"Does that also mean you don't want the goods and services the Enclave will provide?" Stalker asked, pointing his rifle at the ground.

"Like what?"

"Food, medicine, demolition of the ruined buildings and new homes for families.

111

Restored communications and utilities to your homes. Does your group have a leader or council?

Chapter Twelve

"I am the leader of the Remonta Territory," the dark bearded man said. "I am Jax James."

"If we can all put away our weapons, I can give you some more details about what the Enclave can do for you and what they require in return."

"I knew it couldn't be that easy," Jax snorted. "But, yeah. We'll hear what you have to say." That was the signal for his man to put away their weapons or lower them if they didn't have a holster for them.

Stalker shouldered his rifle, and Neely holstered her pistol.

"I think you'll find that most of their requirements are reasonable and self-explanatory," said Stalker as he retracted his helmet and asked Neely to retract hers. "How many of you have families?"

"Most of us do, but it's not easy keeping them fed and safe from the other gangs," said Jax.

"We can definitely help with that. We'll set up a supply drop with food and supplies within your community. Then we will send in techs with protectors to work out a plan for demolition and constructing homes with amenities such as electricity and indoor plumbing.

"They will assist you in setting up a government for your town and help you become self-sufficient by growing your own food and developing small industry to make things to sell and trade with other towns."

"That all sounds great. What's the catch?" Jax demanded.

"The Enclave forbids human trafficking, slavery, stealing, murder, protection schemes to name a few. The com-tablet I will give you can access all that information. It responds to voice commands and will read the information aloud if you can't read it yourself. Do any of your people know how to read?"

"Some," Jax said.

"As your community is rebuilt and communications restored, learning centers can be established. These programs have already been established successfully in the East," Stalker continued, taking out a foldable com-tablet. "Right now, we are passing these out to the leaders in each town. As these communities rebuild, Enclave representatives will pass them out to each family."

"Is your Enclave going to do something about the other gangs that raid us and take our women and supplies?"

"That's exactly why I am here... To contact the leaders and assess how many protectors we need to break up those gangs," Stalker replied. "I'll show you how to work the tablet, then you can show me where you want your supplies dropped, and I will get the coordinates from the tablet."

Stalker showed Jax how to turn on the tablet. "Your two main contacts will be Enclave Community Outreach and Law Enforcement. Say your name, please."

"Jax James."

"Now, it will respond to your voice. If you want to add users, you just say it, and the tablet will ask the person to speak their name. You can also ask it how to do things or find out more information about the Enclave programs and the laws that govern their territories."

Stalker then handed Jax the com-tablet. "You can also call for assistance if you are under attack. Just tell it to call law enforcement or me, Stalker Knight." He repeated his name because people often forgot after hearing it only once. "Now, if you show us where you would like your supply drop, we will put in the order and be on our way."

"Come with us," said Jax. "There is a cul-de-sac in the center of our territory.

It was another five-minute walk to Jax's neighborhood. A group of ten rundown bungalows lined a crumbled paved circle. Dirty children dressed in rags played in the dirt in yards that grew spindly-looking vegetable plants.

Women dressed in primitive-looking clothing tied together with cloth strips watched over the children. Stalker looked around at them and frowned. This was not the kind of community he'd pictured for his family in his virtual life.

They lived in broken-down houses with no power or water service. Most of them looked undernourished, including the men.

"Right here where we are standing would be perfect. We'll be here to get it when it comes," said Jax as they stopped in the middle of the circle.

"It will come by drone, and they will probably send you a message with the arrival time," Stalker said. "We'll check back with you the next time we are in the area."

With a nod to the neighborhood leader, he said, "Let's go," and turned back to the way they'd come. Neely fell into step beside him. "Extract your helmet. We don't know what's changed out there since we got here."

Neely nodded and pushed the button on her belt to extend the helmet and faceplate. Stalker did the same as they walked back to where the sky cycle was stashed. They both carried their rifles by the shoulder straps with their hands near their blaster pistols. She instinctively knew not to talk to Stalker as he scanned their surroundings for danger.

Five minutes from their destination, bullets bounced off Stalker. Shrugging off his rifle, he caught it and aimed in a split second. He deliberately fired to the shooter's side on the roof of a building about fifty yards away.

Neely couldn't move as fast as Stalker, but she pulled her rifle down and held it up so she could see through the scope. She spotted the shooter as well but didn't fire. Instead, she did an about-face, scanning the area behind him.

"The shooter on the roof is gone. Let's keep going."

"Are you okay?"

117

"Fine, it bounced off. Now you understand the reason for our armor. I've been shot at nearly every time out," Stalker said and added, "Let's keep going."

Stalker walked backward while Neely moved forward, rifle poised as she scanned their surroundings. No one else shot at them, but they could still hear intermittent gunfire in the distance. It took only a few more minutes to reach the crumbling building where they left the sky cycle.

Inside, Stalker retracted his helmet and indicated Neely should do the same. He stowed his rifle in the sky cycle's sling while Neely went to the other side to put hers in a matching sling. When she straightened, Stalker was standing in front of her.

"Come 'ere." He moved closer and pulled her against him, kissing her in what began as a tender kiss. His arms tightened around her, pressing their armored bodies together while the kiss quickly turned passionate.

Neely slid her arms around his neck, caressing him as his tongue danced with hers. She couldn't feel his erection through their armor, but she didn't doubt it was there as desire surged through her body, alerting her lady parts.

Lost in their kiss, she vaguely wondered if he planned to initiate sex there. As aroused as she was, she had no will to resist. But this was not the time or place. She was both relieved and disappointed, when he pulled back, parting his lips from hers.

"Stalker…" she spoke his name in a breathy sigh, staring into his eyes. Gone was the impersonal commander, replaced by her passionate lover.

"Save that thought for later. I just needed to hold you," he said, resting his forehead against hers. "We're going to find out who was shooting at us and why."

He held her for a few seconds more, then reluctantly released her. Neely smiled at him, realizing she had needed that, too.

Stalker climbed on the bike and pinged his helmet to cover his head. Neely followed his example and climbed on the bike behind him.

"I've pinpointed the building where the shooter was. We're going to investigate. Stay alert."

"Absolutely," Neely assured him.

Stalker tooled the hoverbike a few feet above the remnants of once busy streets. The ancient pavement was cracked and crumbling and partially blocked in many places by debris from bombed-out buildings. After a hundred years, the city and suburbs looked like a war zone where many people had died. There were even skeletal remains in the rubble.

It reminded Stalker of the many worlds he'd fought on in the wake of the Mesaarkan's destruction. Within days of the first bomb, every major city on Earth was reduced to this. After so many years left on their own, bringing these people back into a semblance of a country would be a monumental task.

He'd been right to put their helmets back up. The closer he got to the shooter's building; the more people were shooting at them.

Stalker stopped the vehicle close to the center of the hidden shooters and called for them to cease firing. His voice was amplified through the console of the sky cycle. He continued by identifying himself and asking to speak to whoever was in charge.

As the shooting stopped, Stalker settled the cycle to the ground and waited. A few minutes later, a tall, bald, dark bearded man emerged from a mostly standing building down the street. He was flanked by four burly-looking men carrying automatic projectile weapons. The apparent leader had a sawed-off shotgun.

Stalker kept his hands on the steering bar grips and retracted his helmet. The five men advanced until they were about ten feet from them.

"I'm Carver Monroe. This is Ashblade territory. Did I hear right? This Enclave is taking over our village?"

"You will still have control over your village, but there are certain laws you must follow," Stalker explained with the authority of his position. "You cannot hold people against their will, nor can you force anyone to perform manual labor or sexual acts, and you cannot buy or sell people for any reason."

Chapter Thirteen

"And who is going to enforce that? You?" Carver asked in a taunting tone.

"Among others…" Stalker replied without emotion. "I'm not here for that today. I'm only here to give you the information. The Enclave can do a lot to improve living conditions with new homes and modern conveniences."

Stalker reached into a pocket and pulled out a folded com-tablet. The four men flanking Byron raised their weapons, aiming them at him. He suppressed a smirk; they had no idea that he could be on top of them before they could even pull their triggers.

"Satellite communication has been restored for the world. I have a com-tablet for you so you can contact the Enclave directly. It's voice-operated if you don't read or write," he said with a passive expression, pretending he didn't know they were trying to decide if they could take him or not.

Stalker swung his leg over the front of the bike and took a couple steps toward them, holding the tablet out so they could see it. They lowered their weapons again, but without engaging the safety switches. He showed Carver how to use it and set it to recognize that man's voice, handing it to him when he finished.

"Is that a female you have on the back of your machine?" Carver asked with undisguised interest. Neely's body armor adhered to her figure, outlining her ample breasts.

Neely's hand went to her blaster's grip, which was currently set on heavy stun.

Stalker went very still. "I think that's obvious." His tone was calm and controlled. "What is your interest?"

"Some of my men need mates, and they are willing to share."

"I am not."

"She is yours?"

"We are mates."

"Can we at least have a look at her?"

"To what purpose?"

Carver's men raised their guns again and pointed them all at Stalker.

"To see if we want her or not," said Carver smugly. Apparently, he thought they could intimidate Stalker with their projectile weapons.

"You do recall that I am a *cyborg* ranger?" he said, hearing Neely pull her weapon from its holster.

"That don't mean nothing to us," Carver said, pointing his shotgun at Stalker.

Stalker considered that these people didn't know about cyborgs because communications had been lost generations before they were born.

Deciding to teach them, Stalker stepped forward, wresting the shotgun from Carver and hitting him in the midsection with the butt. He hit the man beside him in the head with the gun and grabbed his weapon, kicking the gun from the man beside him. Pivoting, he smashed the shotgun into the fourth man's head, grabbed his weapon, tossed it aside, and punched the fifth man.

"It doesn't matter if you want her or not." Stalker picked up the guns and flung each one of them away as hard as he could. "She has chosen me… Only me!"

All five men lay on the ground groaning while Stalker strode back to his bike, swinging his leg over the handlebar to mount it. Setting it in motion, he headed to the next stop.

"You didn't have to do that," said Neely, sliding her arms around his waist. "I can take care of myself, you know."

"It was an emotional response. I needed to educate them."

Neely chuckled. "It was fun to watch." She tightened her arms around him and rested her helmet against his back.

The next place they went, they were also greeted by armed men.

As they landed, Neely said, "Let me come with you, and we can approach them together as law enforcement partners."

That group welcomed them once they learned about their mission. Someone had taken women from their community. Since they weren't that far from Carver's gang, it was logical to suspect they were responsible.

Stalker ordered a supply drop and left them a com-tablet. They still had a week before the cyborg reinforcements arrived.

The next place they approached; the shooting started before they even stopped. Stalker gunned the bike and took them to cover behind a building. Even though bullets couldn't penetrate their armor, they could

125

possibly damage his sky cycle, and it was a ninety-mile walk home.

They both got off the bike and pulled out their rifles. Stalker stepped out into the open, drawing their fire while he scanned the area to pinpoint where they were. About a dozen of them were all on top of buildings in a semi-circle around them.

The main concentration of people in this gang was a half-mile away. He needed to get behind them and pick them off with his blaster on stun. Killing people was not going to solve the problem.

"Neely, I'm going to circle around and neutralize them. I want you to stay here and fire at them intermittently to keep their attention on you. Use the low setting. We are not supposed to kill anyone if we can avoid it."

"Okay, I can do that."

Neely moved to the edge of the building and fired off a couple bolts in the direction of the attackers. Every time someone shot in her direction, she fired back. She felt the impact of bullets hitting her armor a few times, but there was no pain.

Minutes passed, and the gunfire became more intermittent. Neely could only guess that

Stalker had neutralized some of the shooters. As things grew quieter, she had the sudden urge to turn around.

She was not fast enough. One of the two males was close enough to grab her rifle and wrench it from her grasp before she could fire. Her effort to pull it back caused her to fall backward.

Neely tumbled into a backward roll and came up with her blaster aimed at them with two hands. She shot them both on heavy stun, and they crumpled. Holstering her blaster, she ran and grabbed her rifle, and went to the cycle to get some zip cuffs from the cargo compartment. She wasn't giving them a chance to sneak up on her again.

The shooting had stopped, so she returned to her spot, holding her rifle pointed at the ground and waiting.

Stalker used his finely honed assassin skills to sneak up on the shooters. He stunned the first four before they even knew he was there. The fifth one spotted him in his peripheral vision and sent a bullet slamming into Stalker's chest.

The cyborg barely noticed as he continued toward the male, grabbing him by the throat and yanking the semi-automatic away with his other hand. Lifting the man up so his feet were off the ground.

The man choked, trying to breathe while trying to pry Stalker's hand off his throat.

"Who is responsible for this attack?" Stalker demanded, lowering him to the ground and loosening his hold just enough so he wouldn't pass out.

"Vradin Blackwood," he rasped.

"Where will I find this Vradin Blackwood?"

"Th-that brick building over there."

The building looked like an old store with the front window spaces covered with boards.

Stalker let him crumple to the ground, then went to the two-story building's roof edge and jumped to the ground. Sprinting to the brick building, Stalker nearly pulled the door off its hinges when he pulled it open. He strode into the building like he owned it.

"Stop right there," said a large muscular male with a heavy beard, pointing a shotgun at his chest.

Stalker kept coming at him, and the male fired almost point-blank. The impact pushed Stalker back a step, but he recovered quickly.

Wresting the weapon out of his grasp, Stalker gripped the male's throat, squeezing it until he could barely breathe.

"Where's Vradin Blackwood?"

Unable to speak, the male pointed toward the back of the building. Stalker released him, and he fell to his hands and knees, gasping.

The first room he had entered was probably the showroom for whatever goods were once sold there. Empty shelves lined the walls, and the doorway to the next room was flanked by display cases with cracked glass. The place was filthy, with a visible layer of dirt on everything.

Stalker opened the door to the next room and found it much cleaner. A man sat at a wooden desk at the back of the room, eating. At least he was until Stalker opened the door without knocking and stepped inside.

"Who the hell are you?"

Stalker didn't answer until he was standing in front of the table and had retracted his helmet. "I am Stalker Knight, cyborg ranger and law officer for the Civil Restoration Enclave of North America. The war is over, and I was sent to bring California back into the united territories. You Vradin Blackwood?"

129

The man stared at him, apparently considering whether he should answer or not.

"Yeah, I'm Vradin. You must have been what all the shooting was about."

"Apparently. My partner and I were just cruising by, looking for whoever was in charge. And suddenly, a hail of bullets rained down on us." Stalker stood looking at him with a grim expression and his hands resting over his hipbones above his gun belt.

"Are you telling me they will come in here and take over?" Vradin frowned.

"The towns will remain mostly autonomous, but there are a few laws they must abide by. We're discovering certain factions are infringing on human rights, as in human trafficking, even outright slavery. That will not be tolerated."

"You think you and your partner can enforce that?" Vradin asked.

Stalker flashed a derisive smirk. "Right now, I'm just the messenger. I've brought you a com-tablet so that you can communicate with the Enclave and learn how the United Territories will be governed. They are more than willing to help restore your infrastructure, provided you cooperate." He took out a tablet from a pocket in his armor.

Unfolding it, he turned it on and showed the screen side to Vradin. "The Enclave offers supplies and medicine. They will send teams to demolish the ruined buildings and construct new homes for your people," Stalker explained, flipping through screens showing the supply drops and the reconstructed towns.

"Before the war, Los Angeles and the surrounding suburbs were one of the most heavily populated places in the world. But no longer. So instead of a massive urban center, it is reduced to a series of small towns. As long as you follow the basic laws on human rights, the Enclave will leave you alone. If not, we will take you down."

Chapter Fourteen

"Do you even know who you are talking to?" Vradin asked. "I own the towns in this section, not just this one. I've got a thousand enforcers protecting my interests and administering my orders. How many rangers have you got?

"Six…." Stalker grinned. "But a hundred more cyborg protectors are on their way. I know that doesn't sound like a lot, but you have no idea what a few cyborgs can do against men only armed with projectile weapons."

"Bring 'em. If your Enclave thinks I will give up everything I have worked for all these years, for supplies and new buildings, they don't know who they're messing with."

"My partner and I just neutralized fifteen of your enforcers."

"You killed my men?" His eyes widened in shock and anger.

"No, they will live. I simply stopped them from shooting at us," Stalker said. "Since you've decided not to cooperate, tell me which other towns are under your rule, and I won't waste my time with them."

"Or maybe you'll decide to neutralize them, too," Vradin replied with a suspicious glint in his eyes."

"I don't understand why you have a problem with laws intended to protect human freedoms. Slavery and human trafficking are non-negotiable." Stalker shook his head at Vradin's stubborn expression.

"I've given you the information." Stalker showed Vradin how to turn on the tablet and access the Enclave's restoration program information and who to contact to set up a supply drop. Momentarily, he received a call from Neely on their com-links.

"Are you okay?" she asked.

"Yes, I'm on my way." To Vradin, he said, "I have to go, but I will check back to see if you change your mind. If we are met with bullets, there will be consequences."

Stalker extracted his helmet, turned, and left. Cyborgs were pretty hard to kill, but their eyes were vulnerable to high power bullets even though their eye socket was reinforced. It shouldn't have been long enough for any of Vradin Blackwood's henchmen to recover and start shooting again; he wasn't taking any chances.

133

Neely was looking through the scope of her rifle to see what was going on in her surroundings. The only movement she saw was Stalker striding back toward her. She retracted her faceplate as he approached and smiled at him.

"Nice job!" Stalker praised as he noted the two males lying bound by their hands behind their backs. He didn't miss the way her face lit with his praise. It chased away his annoyance with Vradin Blackwood and the prospect of further hassles that lay ahead as he reconned the area for law enforcement.

Focusing on his mate, his thoughts turned to taking her home and breeding her senseless. His stiffening cock liked the idea. Neely looked delectable in the armor that hugged and accentuated all her curves.

"Let's go home. I've had enough of ignorant people today."

"What about them?"

"We'll take off the cuffs and leave them."

"They tried to assault me."

"But you won." He gave her a sexy smirk. "Anyway, the nearest jail is in New Chicago."

"Got it. We don't have any way to get them there or a place to keep them until transport can come to get them." Neely hunkered down and released the cuffs on each man. They'd been unconscious for a long time, so she checked for a pulse, and they were both still alive.

"Let's go home," Stalker said as he walked to the sky cycle. He stashed his rifle in its sling and climbed on, waiting while Neely stowed the cuffs and her rifle. When she had settled in the seat behind him, he started the engine.

Sending it hovering straight up high over the treetops, he morphed the vehicle into flyer mode, pivoted northward, and gunned it toward home.

After landing the sky cycle inside the garage, Stalker and Neely went straight to the weapons room to stow their weapons and Neely's armor belt. As Neely returned her belt to its case, she glanced up to find Stalker naked with his cock fully engorged. She smiled at him.

"I think I need you to join me in the shower for some heavy breeding." Neeley went to stand in front of him, sliding her hands up around his neck and leaning into him.

"Exactly what I had in mind."

Stalker gripped her waist and lifted her up against him, chest to chest, and Neely lifted her legs to curl around him. Taking the opportunity to cup and squeeze her buttocks, he looked into her eyes, his own smoldering with lust.

They pressed their lips together in a passionate kiss as Stalker hugged her to him, basking in her tenderness as their tongues swirled in a sensual dance. Each savored the warm pressure of body against body.

Neely was beginning to admit that Stalker was starting to feel like home. She had glimpsed raw emotion more than a few times when he was watching her and didn't seem to notice she had seen.

She was also more sexually attuned to him than she had ever been with anyone. He was all alpha when he fucked her long and hard, and she loved it.

Stalker had already started toward their en suite before their kiss had finished. He set her on her feet inside the bathroom and helped her take off the thin undergarment she wore under her armor. The shower started with a fine mist as he lifted her and pressed her against the smooth stone tile wall.

Neely wrapped her arms around his shoulders and her legs around his hips.

Feeling her slick against his belly, he found her entrance with the tip of his cock and slid it into her, causing them both to groan in pleasure. He always seemed to know if she needed foreplay to take his cock.

Sometimes, she only had to look at him and remember how he could make her feel, and she would be wet for him.

Now that she was situated, Stalker slid his hands between them and tweaked and rolled her nipples between his fingers, watching her face. Neely didn't hide her pleasure as her inner walls contracted around his cock. Slowly thrusting in and out, he kissed her face, dragging his lips over her jawline to her earlobe.

She moaned as he sucked on her earlobe and nibbled it while teasing her nipples. After a few more thrusts, he kissed his way down her neck to the sensitive spot where her neck met her shoulder. Kissing his way back up to her mouth, he claimed her lips hungrily in a deep passionate kiss.

During the kiss, he pinched her nipples to the edge of pain, which shot frissons of pleasure to her core. Water rained down on them harder, mostly hitting Stalker's back while he moved to cup her buttocks with his hands.

Thrusting at a slow and steady pace, Stalker held her lips, hostage to his plundering. He gradually picked up the pace until he rammed his cock into her hard and fast, chasing that mutual orgasm to ecstasy.

Neely huffed and moaned, clinging to his shoulders and digging her heels into his ass as their hips slammed together. In… Out… In… Out… There was such joy in how their bodies came together and pulled back to come together again.

Stalker took her through two orgasms before he came on her third. Neely keened as his hot semen poured into her, and she jerked with the contractions his pulsing cock sent through her body.

It was so good! …Because it was Stalker. Neely could not help feeling tenderness and affection for this cyborg male who was attentive to her pleasure.

Her attraction to him was just as powerful as that first day, maybe even more so. Yet it was more than that. They were becoming friends as well as lovers. She was slow to understand that she didn't have to guard her feelings in her relationship with Stalker. He was committed to loving her as his lifemate.

He almost seemed to love her unconditionally, if that was possible. That they were genetic mates was all he needed to know.

They kissed and caressed for a time as their orgasms waned and finally separated. Rinsing off under the shower spray, Stalker took the precious shampoo and proceeded to wash Neely's hair. Then he took the cottage industry bar soap, rubbing it into the washcloth until it was coated with thick suds. He used it to wash her from head to toe, dragging it over her body, so it almost felt like foreplay.

Neely did the same for him while he washed his own hair because he was too tall for her to do it well. By the time they were rinsed and dried; they were primed for another round of sex in their bed.

Neely was still asleep when Stalker woke her by shaking her upper arm. She groaned sleepily. "Is it time to go already? I feel like I just went to sleep."

"Because you did, sweetheart. I have to go help Darken raid a human trafficking operation."

"Hold on, I'll come with you," she said immediately.

"No, it's too dangerous. They already shot Darken's mate. I won't risk losing you. I only woke you to tell you so you would know where I went." He kissed her quickly before she could protest, and he was gone.

It was dawn, but their bedroom was still dark. They had made love deep into the night, and Neely admitted to herself she wasn't up for a ride to the east coast, let alone for a raid. She worried briefly for his safety, but he was a cyborg. He'd fought nearly a hundred years in an interstellar war and lived to save her life.

He would be back... And he was... Thirty-six hours later.

"How did it go?" Neely asked as they carried their dinner plates to the breakfast nook and sat down to eat.

"We killed or captured all the gangers and put them in the holding where they kept all the abductees. Shadow and—" Stalker stopped talking midsentence and stared off into the distance.

Neely sighed, recognizing that look. He often got that look when accessing data from his internal computer or receiving messages through the cyborg net. Sometimes, it was only for seconds. It took longer than that, so Neely started eating the meat and vegetable casserole she had chosen.

When Stalker blinked and shook his head, Neely knew the message had finished. "What's up?" she asked.

"Darken said they found Devlin White dead in his mansion."

"I thought killing overlords was tabu."

"It is. Darken and Captain Savage recorded him alive when they left."

"So, who killed him?

"You should finish eating before I show you what they found. It's not pretty."

"Okay, so… Where were you while this was going on?"

"Outside securing the compound and freeing the abductees so we could lock up the gangers we didn't have to kill. Once we finished that, Protectors from the eastside of Enclave territory came to finish up, and we

141

left. I spent as much time traveling as I spent onsite."

"Was it as chaotic as it sounds?"

"Only among the gangers. We had it under control," said Stalker, pausing to take a bite of food.

"I know you weren't gone that long, but I missed you."

Stalker reached across the small table and cupped her cheek with his hand. "I sure didn't want to be away from you any more than necessary." He smiled, stroking her cheek with his thumb.

Chapter Fifteen

Stalker had already transferred the video from White's mansion to his tablet. They took their tea into the living room and sat together on the couch to view it together.

"Remember, I warned you," he said, starting the replay:

Devlin White's body hung from a set of manacles against a wall and his head sagged from apparent exhaustion. But he was alive and breathing.

Finally, he stood and held his head up. Someone walked into the room, but the recording only showed him from behind. White clearly recognized him; his next words confirmed it.

"Price, where the hell have you been? The place was overrun with cyborgs last night; you should have been here!"

"You sent me to kill Darken Wolf," said Colton Price. "I went looking for him."

"You're a cyborg, for Chrissakes! Don't you have a network you tap into? Darken Wolf was right here with the rest of them? Where the fuck were you?"

Colton stopped in the middle of the room and stood looking at Devlin. "Only manufactured cyborgs are on that network. I'm a convert, remember."

"Yeah, okay. Never mind. Just get me out of this."

"I don't know; it looks like karma to me."

"Fuck you!"

"Now you know how those females felt when you left them right where you are now." Colton walked up to Devlin and reached for the manacles with one hand.

He pulled the combat knife from his weapons belt and thrust it into Devlin just under his breast bone, slanting it upward and twisting it. Devlin grunted, and Colton pulled out the knife and stabbed it into the overlord three more times.

"That's for Tessa!" the cyborg hissed, pulling the knife out, stepping back. "I only wish I had time to make you suffer more, fucking pervert."

Colton started to walk away, but the rage erupting inside him made him turn back and kick Devlin's lifeless form in the nuts.

It seemed like Price knew about the camera in the room. He looked directly into it as he left the room, his expression one of stark anguish.

"Who was Tessa?" Neely asked.

"His mate. She was abducted while Price was away. No one knows what happened to her. They found her flat in Starport city empty. No one has heard from her since over a year ago."

"But that recording clears your team from the murder."

"Yes."

"Poor guy. I almost feel sorry for him. Are they going after him for this?"

"They didn't say, but they will take him into custody if he's found and probably send him to psych rehab. He's served honorably until now."

"What do you think happened to his wife?" Neely asked.

"Someone took her, and it might have been White, or he obtained her from whoever took her. Price apparently believed White killed her, or he would have interrogated him before killing him. That's what I would do."

"Well, I hope you never have to."

Stalker set down the tablet and pulled her onto his lap. "So do I," he said and claimed her lips in a deep passionate kiss, ending the conversation. Minutes later, he carried her into their bedroom and made love to her long and slow.

Twenty-four hours after Stalker returned, he and Neely went back to scouting the ruins of Los Angeles. They handed out com-tablets to the leaders who seemed ready to accept help from the Enclave to improve their living conditions.

Since Neely was an experienced flyer, Stalker agreed when she asked for her own sky cycle. She was a quick study because of her previous skill. Most of the time, Stalker and Neely shared his cycle, and other times they each rode their own, mainly so they could carry more tablets to hand out.

Within the once-great city there were completely razed areas where buildings were pulverized to a pile of rubble. It almost seemed the Mesaarkans had bombed it more heavily than other world population centers.

In other areas, there were buildings with minimal damage. Millions had died in the bombings, and more died in the aftermath.

Life as they knew it was over. There was no more running water to their homes, no electricity, no internet, and no mass communication. Retail outlets that weren't reduced to rubble were looted in the first months until nothing was left.

Most of the megalopolis dwellers had no idea how to survive without the amenities of modern life. People who did survive gravitated to others who knew how to get food and water in primitive conditions after the bombing.

Vradin Blackwood's ancestors had become leaders in the aftermath, gaining power by helping others learn how to survive in the new primitive conditions. Perhaps, in the beginning, it was a benevolent relationship with the people who gravitated to their leadership.

By the time Vradin Blackwood ascended to leadership, he'd become an overlord dictator ruling over a dozen communities surrounding the original one founded by his ancestors.

While they still had vehicles that worked, they went out into the countryside and gathered livestock and corralled them in green spaces in the city. They salvaged old books from abandoned houses still intact enough to go inside. Books on survival, hunting, homesteading, and raising livestock were among the most valued.

With the mass destruction of the cities went the financial system. While there was still physical currency, it wasn't very useful when they could no longer simply buy the things they needed.

Vradin Blackwood's predecessors had a knack for stockpiling those things. Those who had nothing to barter would provide services, labor, or sexual favors.

After another long day scouting the city ruins and meeting with people who lived there, Stalker pinged their food processor to prepare dinner for them. Two steamy trays of meat and vegetables awaited them when they arrived, along with covered mugs of hot tea.

"Did you have any idea what you were getting into here?" Neely asked as they carried their food to the small table in the kitchen.

"Hypothetically, but the reality is more than I processed. Out of forty million living here before the war, I have estimated only about a million left." He sat his tray and mug on the table, and Neely did the same.

"They're spread out all over the place," Neely said, collecting tableware from the counter dispenser to her right. She passed Stalker a knife, fork, and spoon and sat down.

"The planners at the Enclave have mapped out how they will spread the communities through the region," Stalker said. "We just have to figure out who might get in the way of those plans."

"Like Vradin Blackwood." Neely took some meat and vegetables on her fork, lifting them to her mouth.

"And others like him." Stalker sipped his tea.

They continued eating and drinking intermittently as they talked.

"At least they stopped shooting at us in his territories, and we've been able to talk to the people inside them," Neely remarked. "I did get the impression not all were happy with their circumstances."

"He makes them pay for his protection. He has his thugs take their best produce and livestock, or they pay in crafts they make to swap for food," said Stalker.

"Do you think he's behind the kidnappings?"

149

"If he is, I haven't figured out where he keeps them."

"Could he be taking them back East like the people Darken was tracking?"

"We have no evidence of working transport vehicles, but the overlords in the East could send a transport."

"Didn't you say Darken used spy drones to track them?" Neely asked.

"He only had specific areas to watch. However, I can request satellite surveillance to see what traffic is crossing the continent," he said. "But we could use a 'fly on the wall' drone in Blackwood's headquarters to find out just how unscrupulous he is."

"Women and children have disappeared in his territory, too. Do you think he's behind that too?"

"He thinks they belong to him, so it stands to reason that he believes he can use them however he wants." Stalker paused, staring into space.

Neely had learned that meant he was receiving info through the cyborg network. She waited patiently for the seconds it took for him to receive the information.

"Good news." His pleased expression told her as much before he even spoke. "The Enclave and Commander Dark agree that California is more than one ranger can handle because of the size of the population."

"That makes sense," Neely agreed, sipping from her mug of tea. "Who are they sending North?"

"Max Steel. They are sending experienced protectors to the northern states. The additional protectors for us are arriving tomorrow. They have chosen to set up at an old military base not far from here. Demolitions and construction teams are moving in after that."

"Where will they even start?"

"Near Jax's area," said Stalker. "I recommended it."

"I'm not surprised." Neely couldn't help smiling at him. "I saw your face when you saw all those kids and how they are living."

Stalker fell silent, and his serious expression made her frown.

"What?"

"The tiny drones are in short supply. It will be a month or more before we can get some from offworld… I need to do some night stalking… Alone."

"Oh." Neely didn't know what to say. She couldn't hide that she didn't like the idea

Stalker held out his hand to her, "Come over here." He said it gently as a request.

She took his hand, getting up from her chair, letting him pull her around the table to sit on his lap. As she turned to face him, he cupped her cheek.

"Sweetheart, you are doing well on the job with me, but you will be safer here for this excursion," he told her gently. "I would rather leave you on your own here than some place in the ruins."

"But what if something happens to you? I won't be there to help you," she worried.

"I'll send you the feed from my internal processor. I can move a lot faster alone because of my enhancements," he said gently.

Neely sighed and gave him a faint smile. "You're right. It will be easier for you to sneak around in the dark without me tagging along trying to keep up."

Before she could say anything else, Stalker kissed her. If Neely knew he was trying to distract her, she didn't object. His kisses were delectable and stimulating. Once they got started, they would usually end up naked and fucking somewhere in the house.

Neely found no will to resist, and it was no longer just pheromone-driven. In the weeks since Stalker had pulled her from her burning flyer, she had fallen in love with him.

She had known from the beginning that there would be times that Stalker would need to work alone. Her armor had a night vision filter, but Stalker's night vision was better.

"When will you go?" she asked between kisses.

"Tomorrow at sunset. We won't go to the city during the day."

Neely was about to say something else, but Stalker didn't seem interested in conversation any longer as he kissed her lightly before claiming her lips in a deep passionate kiss.

While kissing her, he untucked her t-shirt from her cargo pants to slide his hands up underneath to knead her breasts and tease her nipples. She made kitten sounds in her throat, letting him know she liked the way he was touching her.

She could feel his erection under her bottom as they kissed. "I feel your arousal," she whispered when their lips parted. "Do you wish to breed?"

"Would that please you?" he asked.

"Very much," she said, caressing his cheek.

Stalker slid his arm under her legs and lifted her as he stood. Pinging the cleaning droid to clear the table, he carried her to their bedroom.

He stripped them both naked in seconds, following Neely into bed, taking her into his arms to prelude breeding.

Neely was everything to him. He had waited his whole life to finally be with her. When he made love to her, he savored their intimacy. He kissed and caressed and fucked her with careful attention to her pleasure. He knew ecstasy when he was inside her, pouring his seed into her.

All he had done and endured had brought him to her, to love *her*…

Chapter Sixteen

Neely had put on a brave face after he kissed her before leaving for Los Angeles, though he knew she didn't want him to go. Leaving her was hard. They had been nearly inseparable for almost two months. Stalker was virtually certain she loved him.

It was in her eyes… how she kissed him and smiled at him. There was tenderness in the way she touched him and pleasured him.

Sometimes, since she became his mate, he wished he didn't have this enormous job of bringing law and order back to this great city. Fortunately, help was on the way. As he approached the city, he realized he was looking forward to stalking again.

He morphed the sky cycle back into its hover bike form and landed by the same abandoned building to stash it. He programmed his armor to a dark matte gray and got off the bike. He hadn't brought his ion rifle because he could move more freely without it.

He had two blaster pistols, various knives, and a shock stick that could be used as a baton or shock an assailant unconscious. In reality,

Stalker probably needed no weapons at all to defend himself.

With his hover cycle safely stowed and cloaked, Stalker went out into the night. Staying in the shadows of tattered buildings, he ran, his footfalls barely making a sound.

When he got to Vradin Blackwood's place of business, Blackwood and another man were coming out of the building. Stalker stopped and hid in the dark doorway in a wall where the rest of the building was a pile of rubble.

"Now that we have a full load when will we ship them?" the man asked Blackwood.

"I should have the date once they've approved the merchandise," said Blackwood. I just transmitted the data and the pictures this afternoon.

"I think Larry is bringing in a couple more kids from up north, probably tomorrow."

"That's good. The Mesaarkans like them young. They make better pets. Is Sam taking good care of them? They don't take sick ones."

"He scanned them, and the alien medic approved them all, but one of the females is pregnant. Sam didn't think she knew yet."

"They'll take her anyway. They can still fuck her."

"Ugh! I almost feel sorry for them. Those Mesaarkan lizards are ugly."

"I don't. They are just human trash, and they will never be anything but scavengers. If they don't die fighting for scraps of food, they'll die fighting over a female."

"I know, but thinking about them fucking a human woman creeps me out."

Stalker let them get further away before he followed them. This was even worse than he imagined. Human trafficking to the Mesaarkans was an abomination. There were anecdotal instances of the aliens taking humans on the worlds they raided, but no hard evidence.

The question now was; where were they keeping the people they captured?

Stalker continued following them.

"With the weapons, they're sending us, we can run those cyborgs out of here. Nobody won the war, you know. It ended because the Wholaskans convinced them to stop fighting."

"I heard what that ranger told Jax from the Remonta clan that the Enclave has thousands of cyborgs to help them on their mission to re-civilize North America," Blackwood's underling told him.

They stopped in front of a brick building set off by itself. Somehow, it seemed to have come through the bombings unscathed. It was surrounded by crumbling asphalt, so it might have been some kind of public gathering spot. It was lit inside, and Stalker noted there were solar panels on the roof.

"You going to relieve Sam, now?" Blackwood asked as they stopped in front of the brick structure.

"Yeah, he wants some time with his female. Do you think the aliens would mind if I tried one of the females? It's been a while…."

"Only if you can do her without damaging her. We need those weapons to keep those cyborgs out of our business."

Stalker stifled a growl, waiting for Blackwood to go inside so he could follow his lackey to where the abductees were being held. While he waited, he sent Neely a message through his internal computer to let her know what he had learned so far.

Finally, Blackwood went inside, and the other man headed down the crumbled road.

Stalker followed at a discreet distance while keeping him in sight. He wasn't hard to track because he seemed to be in no hurry.

After about ten minutes, they came to what was once a group of buildings with only one still standing. The upper stories were damaged, but the ground floor appeared to be intact.

The unnamed flunky stopped at the door and knocked in a three, then two knocks sequence.

Stalker grabbed his stun baton and ran up behind the other man, jabbing him in the back. He grunted as the shock coursed through his body, slumping to the ground. Pulling the body back, Stalker stood, his back against the wall, beside the doorway.

The door opened. "Is that you, Ken? What the hell?" The man Stalker presumed to be Sam took a step toward the unconscious man, and Stalker zapped him, grabbing his arm to break his fall.

He probably could have punched them out with his fist, but Stalker weighed that stunning them was less likely to kill them. He might need to question them later. As he slipped inside, the hallway was dimly lit.

There was a chair and a desk with some leftover food on it.

Stalker scanned the building and found about fifty people divided into twelve rooms. He could hear some talking among them, and some were crying.

Most of the doors had small windows so he could look inside the darkened rooms. They were unfurnished, with women and girls lying on cloth pallets. Two rooms held men, and two had young boys. Each was fastened shut on the outside with metal hasps with a straight bar shoved through the hole. Primitive but they worked.

One of the rooms with a crude lock was empty, so Stalker carried the unconscious men to it and locked them inside. His next impulse was to let their captives out of their cells and reassure them, but that would only bring chaos to the situation.

This is where Neely could help him. Dawn was hours away, so it should be safe for Neely to come out.

Neely snatched up her com-tablet as soon as it beeped. She was surprised to see Stalker's face rather than a text message.

"Hey, beautiful."

Neely grinned at him. "What's happening?"

"I found the abductees. Blackwood has them locked up in an old school building. They're confined to rooms right now. I could use your help coordinating with them."

"Just tell me, where. I'll be there in twenty. Sounds like a prelude to trouble; I'll bring your rifle."

"The protectors will be here at dawn. They will transport them to the military base, and then we will go after Blackwood's gang."

"I'm on my way," Neely told him. "See you soon."

Before they even finished the conversation, she was going to the weapons room for her armor/weapons belt. Stripping off her regular clothing, she donned the tank top and shorts that went under her armor. Fastening the belt around her, so it rested at her hip bones. She pressed the button that unleashed her armor.

She pulled out two blasters, holstered them, and fastened her shock wand to her belt. Grabbing their ion rifles, she strode out to the garage and slid them into the slings on her sky cycle. Everything else she might need, including a change of clothing, was in the cargo compartment.

Turning around in the garage, she eased the hover bike out onto the lawn and set it to rise vertically until it was above the tree tops. She morphed it into a sky cycle and shot off into the night sky.

Neely arrived at the old school building in exactly twenty minutes since Stalker commed. She had hoped she would see some action after all the training they did those past few months, so she was a little disappointed that Stalker called her in to handle the victims. Yet, it was better than sitting at home, a bundle of nerves, because she didn't know what was happening.

Setting her sky cycle down at the side of the building in the shadows, she cloaked it then extracted her helmet and commed Stalker to let him know she was there. He was in the open doorway of the building when she came around the corner carrying both of their rifles.

Taking his rifle and shouldering by its strap, he smiled at her, beckoning her to come inside.

Neely smiled back, wondering how the man could look so damn sexy without even trying. But they weren't here for that, she sighed to herself.

Then he surprised her and pulled her in close for a slow, sexy kiss.

"Save that thought for when we're done here," he whispered in her ear afterward.

Neely just smiled and stroked his cheek.

Chapter Seventeen

"You mean these bastards are selling the people they take to the Mesaarkans? The same guys you fought for nearly a century?" Neely blurted as she finished playing back the vid on her com-tablet.

"Yes. When I heard that, I wanted to end him then and there. Selling humans to the Mesaarkans after all they have done to our world... After all, we suffered protecting our people...."

"But you needed to find the stolen people first."

"He's going to prison. They opened one on Penta about fifty years ago. No guards and no rules."

"Are the Mesaarkans really lizards?" Neely asked.

"They are reptilian humanoids, bipedal with scales and a long lizard-like tail. They are physically capable of mating with human females, but I had never heard of them doing so until now."

"How much longer before the protectors arrive?" Neely asked.

"They will be here sooner than expected, about an hour. We're going to load these people into the troop transports and send them to the old military base, then we raid Blackwood's and his gangers' homes."

Neely knew she wouldn't like what he would say next when he paused after that.

"I want you to go with them."

"Oh, come on, Stalker! We've trained for weeks. How can I get any field experience if you send me away before anything goes down?"

"I just don't want you hurt. Worrying about you getting hurt will distract me."

"What about me? Don't you think I will worry about your safety? You are a tough cyborg, but you're not quite invincible." She paused for a moment gathering her thoughts. "You're going to have protectors outside securing the perimeter. Let me do that."

Stalker frowned, and a muscle in his jaw twitched as he ground his teeth while running probabilities through his internal processors.

It seemed riskier to damage her esteem for him than to damage her physically if he let her observe outside. She worked hard to learn the job, both physically and intellectually.

"Okay," he said finally. "You can shadow one of the protectors outside. I will lead the team inside. We are breaking in without warning. If he is communicating with the Mesaarkans, he will have contact with his gangers.

"I'm sending protectors to the ones we know about, but raiding Blackwood's house should be finished before many can get here."

Neely nodded. "Then I guess we better get these people ready to leave as soon as the protectors arrive."

They went to the first room holding women and girls. Stalker unlocked the doors and opened them, letting in light from the hallway. Immediately they heard moans and whispering.

"You leave these girls alone, you pervert!" one of the adult women asserted.

"Everyone stay calm. I am Cyborg Ranger Stalker Knight and with me is my mate, Neely. We are here to rescue you. We have transport coming to take you to safety while we arrest your kidnappers."

"We have people to help make arrangements to get you back to your homes. The Civil Restoration Enclave is taking over this territory. They have plans to remove the damaged structures and build new homes for everyone living here. They will also teach you how to help so you can pull your own weight. Where we are taking you, there are people who will explain the program further and answer any questions you may have.

"We'll leave the door open while we open the rest of the cells. Please don't leave the building until the hover crafts arrive to evacuate you."

They went to eleven other rooms for Stalker to give the rescue speech. The last room had ten little boys between ages four and nine. The smallest started to cry because he didn't know where he lived or where his mommy was.

Neely was about to comfort him when a woman down the hall cried "Donnie!" and came running. She was hardly more than a girl. She slipped into the room between Stalker and Neely to scoop the little boy up into her arms. "Oh, baby, I was so afraid they left you there on your own."

More women came down to learn if their boys had been captured. All but one of the boys was spoken for. He was about six years old and of mixed heritage. He stood off on his own, stoically watching the reunions. Neely went over to him.

"Hi, my name is Neely. What's your name?"

"Manny," he said. "They took my brother away after we got here. We don't have a mother anymore. Bad men killed her."

"What's your brother's name?"

"His name is Jorge."

With all the cells open, the captives began to mingle and talk as they looked for friends and relatives. Even shouting for him would do little good because of the noise.

Neely offered the boy her hand, and he took it. "Let's go look for him."

"Okay."

As they walked between the little huddles of people, Neely counted the rest of the people. There were thirty women and girls, ten little boys, and fifteen males in their teens and twenties. A few had gone over by the women, and a few girls had gravitated toward the teenage boys.

Jorge wasn't among them, so Neely took Manny with her to check all the cells to make sure everyone was out. They found him on a pallet in the third room. The boy recognized his brother immediately. Slipping his hand from Neely's, he hurried to Jorge's side.

"Jorge, wake up."

Neely went down onto one knee when Manny got no response and pressed two fingers to his neck to feel for a pulse. It was there, and she could see he was breathing in the dim light.

"Stalker, we found Jorge, but we can't wake him. Can you come to take a look?"

"On my way," he responded immediately and was there in seconds. Scanning the teenager with his internal scanner, he quickly found the problem. "He has a concussion and bruises. Someone beat him, but I think he will recover. The medic will treat him when he arrives. It should only be another twenty minutes. I will contact them to bring in a stretcher for him."

"There are only two choices of who hurt him. Either his roommates or the guards," said Neely.

"I will question them."

Stalker found three teenagers from Jorge's room in the hall to the lobby. They watched him nervously as he approached. Even without his armor and weapons strapped to his body, Stalker appeared formidable.

169

"Can you tell me what happened to the other male in your cell?"

"He went at the guard about his brother. That guard whacked him with his shock stick several times on his body and then in the head."

Stalker assessed his respiration and heartbeat. The young male seemed to be telling the truth. "Thank you. I will add that to his charges."

Only then did they note the circled star embossed in his armor. "What does that star mean," asked one of them.

"I am a law enforcement ranger. The people who kidnapped and held you here have violated your rights. They will be punished."

The medic arrived with the reinforcements exactly twenty minutes after Stalker contacted them. He had the universal nanites to treat the injured boy, whereas Stalker carried only gene-specific for himself and Neely.

The cyborg medic loaded Jorge on the hover stretcher and guided it out to the transport craft with Manny tagging behind him.

Only then did they direct the rest of the captives to three of the transporters ready to take them to the old military base near the mountains. It was far enough from the city that it had escaped all but minor damage in the bombings.

They would use it both to house the cyborgs protectors and technical staff while they did demolitions and built new housing for people living in the ruins. Those residents would also be sheltered at the base while waiting for their new homes' completion. The Enclave planned to add temporary housing near the base to rotate people through as work began in their ruins.

After the captives left, the protectors came inside to hear Stalker's plans for the raids on Vradin Blackwood and his gangers. He shared the coordinates and images of the people they were to capture. They were mostly males, but a small percentage were females as well.

Stalker and Neely had scouted Blackwood's gangers between the meeting and passing out com-tablets to people they oppressed. The plan was quickly distributed to all one hundred cyborgs through their internal network.

As the gangers were captured, additional cyborgs manning the two transporters would bring them to their old holding center to lock them up.

The teams left on foot because they could move stealthily through the neighborhoods. Stalker led his team of five plus Neely to Vradin Blackwood's home.

Chapter Eighteen

As Stalker and his team approached Blackwood's building, they found two armed guards walking the perimeter around it. Stalker was disturbed to discover that they were carrying the Mesaarkan equivalent to their ion rifles.

He was sorely tempted to shoot them on sight because possessing such weapons meant they were traitors to the Federation. Only, they didn't deserve a quick death. Sending them to a lawless prison planet was what they deserved.

Stalker sent two of the protectors to neutralize them with shock sticks.

As soon as the first one fell, an ear-piercing high-pitched alarm sounded unexpectedly. Leaving one of the cyborgs with Neely and another to guard the perimeter, Stalker took the other two into the house.

Blackwood was waiting for them with a Mesaarkan rifle and fired off a couple shots before Stalker stun blasted him. Next, he located the source of the alarm and hacked the AI to silence it—more Mesaarkan tech.

Once the alarm was silenced, a woman screamed, "Help! Somebody help me!"

"I'll go," said Protector Bradix Strong.

Meanwhile, Protector Gunner Max secured Blackwood, zip cuffing his hands behind his back.

"Bradix report."

"Sir, he has a woman tied naked to the bed. She is mine, and she is not here by choice. He's been holding her here and using her. I am cutting her loose now."

"Bring her down when she is ready. We'll transport her back to the base as soon as a hovercraft arrives," said Stalker.

"Sir, we've got incoming flyers," Zevin Linx warned.

Flyers? Stalker wondered for a stunning moment. Neely! He ran to the front doorway, firing off a dozen bolts before he was hit. The aircraft bolt slammed him backward against an inner wall with enough force to knock him out. However, it didn't pierce his armor.

Sustaining heavy damage, the craft pulled up, clipping the rooftop and crashing behind the house.

Two more flyers came out of the ruins. Neely and the two protectors, Hawk and

174

Slater, shot at them. One crashed into the second story plunging through and crashing behind near the one Stalker shot down. The other veered off to the side before it crashed.

Next, a dozen males came out of the rubble, shooting more Mesaarkan rifles. Neely and the two cyborg protectors fired their ion rifles in repeater mode, fanning across the line of shooters advancing on them. They stood out in the open because there was no place to hide.

One of the cyborgs took a hit that knocked him down, but he got right back up. Bolts whizzed by Neely, but she kept firing until the enemies were all down. They were not wearing armor like Neely and the cyborgs.

As the shooting stopped, Neely called for Stalker on her helmet com but got no answer. She turned and ran into Blackwood's home and found him on his back, his head propped against the wall. She knew cold terror as she hunkered down beside him, unable to tell whether he was dead or alive…

Then, he groaned and opened his eyes. He blinked twice and smiled as he met Neely's concerned gaze. "Now, that hurt, but I'm okay," he assured her. "I was afraid for you, out there in the open."

"We took down a defense team armed with some high-tech rifles."

Stalker sat up. "Probably Mesaarkan. Those flyers are. Blackwood must have sold a lot of humans to the Mesaarkans. Fucking traitors," he said, getting up from the floor.

"Bringing in the protectors was a great plan. Without the extra help, we could only take them out a few at a time. Now, I wonder if that eastern overlord Devlin White had connections with Blackwood's gangers."

"Are you thinking that those rifles I was smuggling could have been Mesaarkan rather than Federation?"

"Possibly. Although with the Overlords' Federation connections, they could well have been ours. But the amount of human trafficking seemed pretty rampant for the number of sex workers in any given location. With the starport in Farringay, that would be the area with the most demand for sex workers. The overlords up and down the eastern seaboard were acquiring them for their own use."

"You think they were shipping the rest out of here to trade with the Mesaarkans."

"Exactly. It may have been happening even before the war ended. Mesaarkans numbers were dwindling as much as ours in the war. Maybe they were acquiring them for breeding purposes."

"Can they even produce offspring with humans?"

"They are warm-blooded, but I have no knowledge of testing them for genetic compatibility," he said.

"Maybe you can find out when the prisoners are interrogated."

"I will ask. Right now, I want to go out and check the flyers for survivors… and to see if any are salvageable."

"May I come?" Neely was asking him as her commanding officer rather than her mate.

"Yes. I think everything is under control here."

Blackwood lay on the floor with his hands cuffed behind him. Brandix was in the sitting room with the woman he'd rescued from Blackwood's bedroom. He'd freed her, helped her find clothing to put on, and brought her downstairs before the upper story was nearly obliterated.

The first flyer was intact, but the pilot had fled. The second was a total wreck from being shot and crashing through the building.

Neely turned to see where the third shuttle landed in time to see the pilot taking aim at them with a long gun. The first bolt whizzed by Stalker's head. Neely pulled out her blaster and shot him before he could fire again, only feeling a little guilty that she had reset the pistol to kill.

Holstering the weapon, she turned to Stalker to reassure herself he remained unhurt.

"Thanks, baby," he said. "I'm glad you insisted on coming with me. I knew you were ready, but I was afraid… No terrified I might lose you." He paused, scanning the area by sight and with his internal sensors. Apparently satisfied it was safe, he pulled her against him and hugged her, kissing the top of her head.

It might not have pierced his skull, but the impact could have damaged his processors and organic brain matter. His preoccupation with Neely's safety had put him in danger.

But Neely was so much stronger than he let himself believe. She put on her armor, and took up her weapons, proving how strong and capable she was… And so sexy…

That was enough to make his cock swell. But he willed it back into submission. One of the drawbacks of working with his beloved mate. It was hard to separate his feelings from his job as her supervisor.

Stalker reluctantly set her from his embrace, stifling the temptation to taunt her with what he wanted to do to her when they were home alone again. He had to halt that line of thinking while he processed what he still needed to do.

The protectors quickly replaced the captives they had liberated from the old school building. It was mid-morning when Stalker got Vradin Blackwood back to the makeshift jail. He took him to a room with a table and two chairs to interview him. Sitting him in a chair at the table with his hands still bound behind his back, Stalker sat in the chair across the table from him.

"Why? Why would you sell your people to the Mesaarkans? Do you have any idea how many billions of humans they killed?"

"They aren't my people. They live like filthy animals in the rubble, fighting over scraps of food and rutting with any female they can find whether she wants it or not," Blackwood growled vehemently. "They were all I had to offer. The Eastern Overlords were trading with me first, then I met a middle man for the aliens. Going through him, I got three times the merchandise."

"Who is this middle man?" Stalker demanded.

"He's one of your kind. A cyborg named Colton Price. When we have a full load, I call him, and he sends hover transport to pick them up. Then they drone ship payment in the form of tech and weapons."

"What you have done is treason to the Federation. You and your gangers are going to prison."

"Well, fuck you and the Federation! Where the hell were they when we were down here fighting to stay alive?"

"They—We were out there in the galaxy trying to save humanity on every world they've colonized. Some greedy prospectors were more concerned with the credits they could make on a mining colony than sentient life. They murdered two hundred Mesaarkans and tried to cover it up. Only one escaped.

"The Mesaarkans rained down hell on every human colony they could find, starting with Earth. That you have sold humans to the Mesaarkans for profit warrants no mercy. The only reason I don't kill you… A quick death is more than you deserve. Sending you to Penta Prison Planet is far more fitting."

Seeing no further need for questioning, Stalker stood and came around the table. He gripped Blackwood's upper arm, pulling him to his feet and knocking over the chair. He dragged Vradin Blackwood to an empty cell and pushed him into it after uncuffing him.

Chapter Nineteen

After putting Blackwood in a cell, Stalker went looking for Neely. Even the therapy he received for PTSD didn't make him forget his war experiences. It allowed him to remember but not let it intrude on his daily life.

After the day he'd had so far, he wanted to hold his mate. He found her outside, consoling the female Vradin Blackwood had tied to his bed. She was crying.

"This cyborg says he is my male, that I am his mate. I don't want to belong to any man, I don't want to be touched, and I don't want to fuck anyone," she sobbed.

Neely hugged her and let her cry.

"Rena, it's going to be okay. Cyborgs are not like the men who hurt you. They have been trained to treat women well. Brandix won't force you to do anything. The medics can help you," Neely soothed.

Stalker hung back, waiting.

"Do you need me to ask him to give you some space?" Neely asked when she had calmed and stepped back.

"Could you? I just don't want to be with any man right now," Rena admitted

"I can understand. I thought I didn't want a mate when Stalker came along. He was pretty hard to resist."

Momentarily, a hovercraft came to settle in front of the holding building.

"Here's your ride to the temporary refuge for the ruins' dwellers. I will let Brandix know that you need some time to recover from your ordeal before you are ready to think about a mate. He is stationed here now, so he can afford to give you time to heal. But don't expect him to give up."

"He was really nice. I just can't do this right now. That bastard Blackwood made my life hell."

"You don't need to worry about him anymore. He is going to prison offworld. The refuge will be secured by cyborgs. They won't let anyone hurt you."

"Will I see you again?" asked Rena.

"Oh, yeah," Neely said and smiled at her. "I will come to check on you in a couple weeks. Now that we have help, things are going to start moving faster. The gangers left are either going to join in rebuilding, or they can go off to prison with Blackwood."

Neely walked Rena to the hovercraft and turned around to see Stalker lingering at the end of the building. He was watching her with interest, which brought a tender smile to her lips.

She strolled over to him, and he gripped her upper arms gently and drew her around the corner of the building with him. Taking her ion rifle and shouldering it with his own, he pulled her against him and hugged her.

"Yeah, I needed that too," she murmured against his chest, hugging him back. "I love you."

"And I love you," he replied huskily, laying his cheek against the top of her head with a sigh. "I wish I could take you home and show you just how much I love you right now."

"I'm looking forward to it," Neely said, "but we have to finish up here first." She leaned back to look up at him, cupping her hand against his cheek, love shining in her eyes. "I'm so glad you are in my life."

Stalker turned his head and kissed her palm. "Me, too. We still have five hours left of daylight. The teams are going back into this section to evacuate the residents, so the demolitions can start in two days."

They withdrew from their embrace reluctantly, and Neely took back her rifle. Even though things seemed calm at the moment, there could still be armed gangers around.

As they were walking back, Neely asked, "Did Blackwood tell you who was arranging the sale of the humans to the Mesaarkans?"

"It was Colton Price. Killing Devlin White was personal, but I don't get why he was trafficking humans to the Mesaarkans. Captain Savage got confirmation Price was working for the Federation, but they lost contact with him. He's gone completely rogue."

"He's been pretty edgy since I met him. Selling humans to the enemy—he must have gone over the edge," said Neely.

"Maybe because he was a natural convert, the therapy we did when we were released from service didn't work for him. The Feds are going to investigate. I will notify them about what I learned. If they ever find him, they'll send him to Penta."

Stalker spent the rest of the day interviewing Blackwood's gangers about what they did for him and how they operated. The protector teams patrolled the ruins rooting out more gangers and helping women and children to safety.

Many of the young males who worked for him were unaware of Blackwood's activities. The youngest were just low-level spies for him.

All while attending to his duties, Stalker looked forward to taking Neely home and making love to her long and slow. He wanted to drive her mad with desire and feast on the juices of her lovely pussy until she screamed her pleasure. Then he would give her respite before he fucked her long and hard.

Only things didn't quite work out that way. By the time they got home, Stalker could see Neely was nearly exhausted. After they put away their weapons and her armor, Stalker followed her into the shower. He'd decided to delay his lovemaking plans until Neely had gotten a good night's sleep.

When she stripped off her undergarments, and he'd retracted his armor, she pressed her naked body against his and said, "I need you to take me in the shower."

As she slid her hands up his chest and clasped them around his neck, she raised herself on her toes and turned her parted lips up for a kiss. That was all the invitation Stalker needed. Kissing her, he lifted her up to wrap her legs around his waist, carrying her into the shower stall.

Scenting her arousal, he knew she was ready and slid his cock into her opening. Relishing the feel of her breasts crushed against his chest and her inner walls hugging his cock, he kissed her deeply, his tongue slow dancing with hers as he tweaked her nipples.

Stalker basked in her caresses as she told him without words that he was precious to her, that she loved him. He'd felt sure she loved him before she said the actual words, but hearing them brought him such joy.

He thrust in and out of her slowly. With her in that position, he could hit both her G-spot and clit on the way in.

"Ah, Neely," he said softly when their lips parted. "You've brought more love into my life than I ever dreamed possible. I have so much love for you that I can't even express it all in words."

"I feel it… too… Stalker. I never… believed I would find anyone to love as much as I love you."

187

There were no more words as he took her mouth in another passionate kiss, thrusting harder and faster until he took them both to orgasm together, pumping his hot essence into her womb. It was pure ecstasy in the mists of the shower.

They stayed like that, kissing and caressing for a long time before Stalker turned the shower full-on, and they washed each other. After they finished and dried, Stalker scooped Neely into his arms and carried her to the bed.

After covering her with the sheet, he went to the kitchen to bring her something to eat and drink. When he came back a few minutes later, she was asleep with a little smile on her lips that made him smile, too.

Chapter Twenty

The next day, Stalker and Neely went back to Blackwood's former residence to work on the downed Mesaarkan flyers. Stalker received permission to confiscate and salvage the planes for personal use at his expense.

Stalker was familiar with that model because his team had stolen them more than once to return to their pickup location from assigned operations. Cramming six cyborgs in a four-passenger plane was a tight fit but better than being left behind.

The flyer that crashed through the house's upper story was only good for parts. The second of the three downed only needed a new power relay, and the third had a blown engine.

Stalker ran a comprehensive search on the AI net and found access to a repair manual for flyers written in Mesaarkan. In all the years he spent fighting and stalking them, he and many other cyborgs were fluent in the spoken and written language.

The power relay on the wreck was undamaged, so Stalker pulled it apart and retrieved the part. That took longer than removing the damaged part and replacing it in the other plane.

Neely helped where she could, mostly handing him tools he needed as he asked for them. She had done basic maintenance on her own plane, but the Mesaarkan design was different than anything she had seen before. Stalker explained the various parts and how they worked to propel the vehicle.

The internal diagnostics confirmed the plane was flight worthy when he finished the repair. Next, he loaded a translation program to reset the language to English to make it easier for Neely to transfer her pilot skills to the alien flyer. Lastly, he registered the plane with the Enclave and the shuttle port in New Chicago to avoid having it identified and shot down as an enemy aircraft.

Because Stalker had flown a similar alien craft before, he piloted their first test flight after the repairs. He went through every step with Neely, explaining the differences between her flyer and the controls for flying and landing the Mesaarkan craft.

He landed the flyer by Blackwood's house and switched places with Neely, so she could take it up. She only had to ask Stalker to remind her of the locations of a couple controls. Neely flew north once they were in the air, maxing out the speed and testing evasive maneuvers.

By the time she slowed and turned around, they had almost reached San Francisco.

"Wow, this thing is fast, way faster than my old flyer!" Neely exclaimed.

"Yes, the propulsion system is fifty-eight-point four two percent more powerful than your old model," Stalker commented.

"How did you get them to let us keep it?"

"I just listed how we could use it on the job, in addition for personal use. We just need to maintain it, which we can do by salvaging the other two for parts. This flyer is better than any they can offer us, and we will use it for work at no charge to them."

"Does it bother you that a salvaged alien plane is better than we can buy here?"

"Not really. We still have the technology, but it will be a few years before we have the means to build any here."

"I wonder how many people were sold to get the three of them."

"Four thousand six hundred and fifty-three in the last ten years…. Over six-billion credits worth."

"OMG! I thought the Mesaarkans hated humans. What do you think they are doing with them?"

"Whatever they wish," Stalker said grimly. "It could be anything from pets to science experiments, enslaved people, breeders, or sex objects. They may be genetically compatible with humans. Speculation goes from there to horrific. They are skillful torturers who can inflict excruciating pain with minimal damage."

"Colton Price was in the war. How could he sell humans to the enemy?" Neely asked.

"I can't even guess. All I got from the Federation indicated that he was a double agent investigating human trafficking. His wife Tessa was under Devlin White's protection when she disappeared before Price returned from the war. She disappeared when the fleet was stretched thin enough that she could have been smuggled offworld. Or

Devlin killed her in one of his twisted games."

"Devlin probably got off easy. They'd probably have sent him to the prison planet. I don't think he would have fared well," Neely commented.

"Price will end up there if he's ever caught."

"Does Darken think the people you all rescued were destined for off-world?"

"He didn't then, but Blackwood's revelation makes him think so now."

"I've seen pictures of the Mesaarkans; I don't know many humans who would find either sex attractive."

"I don't know why the Mesaarkans would want humans other than to make them suffer," Stalker replied. "Since we don't have diplomatic relations with them, I don't know how we could find out."

Soon they were back in Los Angeles, landing the flyer by Blackwood's house. Stalker checked in with the protectors, who were busy clearing the adjacent blocks of rubble dwellers. The teams to clear away the ruined buildings would arrive in two days.

193

Meanwhile, Stalker and Neely went back to salvaging parts from the other two wrecked flyers.

After killing Devlin White, Colton Price took the dead man's personal aircraft and flew it to his secret mountain cabin. It was a prefab he'd bought when he returned to Earth after the war, located just east of the boundary between Enclave and Overlord territories.

The only way to reach it is by coordinates in a hover-flyer. His Federation handler could ping his internal computer to locate him, but not without him knowing. The four-room dwelling was nestled in a grove of tall pines that shielded it from view by air.

Price sat on the concrete slab in a folding chair, sipping from a bottle of whiskey he'd snagged from White's private supply. He felt no remorse for killing White. The man was evil in what he did to women.

He still suspected White had killed his wife Tessa or sold her to the highest bidder. White claimed he didn't know what happened. She went missing one day, and the Overlord never heard from her again.

Finding Tessa had been Colton Price's main reason for taking the job as a covert operative for the Federation. But he no longer felt any loyalty to them. He'd given his legs, an arm, an eye, and various organs, fighting for humanity. Rather than let him die, they turned him into an abomination.

Tessa swore it didn't matter. They had loved each other since they were kids. She was thrilled he was alive and coming home. By the time he returned a month later, she was gone without a trace. A year later, he was no closer to finding her.

He put the bottle to his lips and took another swallow relishing how it burned all the way down. Now that he had murdered Devlin White, none of the other overlords would trust him, and the buyers would be pissed because the merchandise had been taken by the cyborg rangers.

Colton couldn't complain to the Federation because even though they didn't have jurisdiction, the people stolen had come from their territory. He was about to take another pull from the bottle when his internal comm bleeped.

"Mr. Price, we have trouble out here. A whole slew of cyborgs raided our territory. They arrested Mr. Blackwood and freed all our merchandise," the ganger told him. "The place is crawling with cyborg protectors, and they are rounding up everyone who worked for Mr. Blackwood. They shot down those alien flyers we had, and they are salvaging them. Blackwood still owes for them. Driscoll is coming for the delivery in two days, and we got nothing."

"Who took the flyers?"

"The new cyborg ranger Stalker Night and his woman."

"Neely."

"Yeah, that's her name. They fixed one with parts from one of the wrecks."

"How the hell did this happen? Blackwood should never have activated those flyers for a ground raid. They were safely hidden. We could have moved them out before they started evacuating the sector."

Colton took another swallow from the bottle as he considered what to do. "Kid, I will call Driscoll and tell him that the Enclave is taking over. We have to move our

196

operations out of North America. I'm coming out to move the weapons before the vat boys find them. Have a nice life if I'm not at the rendezvous in three days."

"What do you mean?"

"There's something I need to do, but it's not a sure thing," Price said cryptically. "If I'm not there, find Driscoll in San Francisco. I'll warn him the cyborgs will be moving in, probably soon."

"Thanks, Mr. Price. Hope you make it."

"I'll do my best." Price stood, picked up his chair, and took it into the house. Time to pack up and leave. With luck, he might be back   someday.

Chapter Twenty-One

Stalker awakened at dawn, even though he and Neely had made love into the wee hours. He wanted to unload the spare parts from the Mesaarkan flyer and put them into the garage until he could build a proper hanger for them.

It was a mundane task he could easily complete alone, so he saw no reason to wake Neely. Most parts were too heavy for her, and he could easily do it himself. He wasn't thinking about intruders or arming himself at his isolated mountain forest home.

He quickly realized his mistake after pulling out a heavy propulsion system piece to find Colton Price pointing a blaster at him. Stalker immediately summoned his armor and heaved the part at Price. The other cyborg deflected the heavy component, and Stalker kicked the weapon from his grasp, going on the offense….

Neely slowly drifted from a dream that was not a dream but a memory of joyful, hot sex with Stalker the night before. She reached for him before she opened her eyes and found his side of the bed empty. With a soft sigh, she opened her eyes and stretched.

Before she finished, the security alarm chimed, and the AI voice announced, "Intruder alert."

A hologram appeared at the end of the bed, showing Stalker battling Colton Price in the front yard beside the Mesaarkan flyer.

Neely jumped out of bed. Passing her hand over a door in the wall on her side, she reached in and grabbed the blaster, checked the setting, and ran from the bedroom naked.

Despite the fact he was wearing his armor, Stalker lay on his back with blood, so much blood seeping from his abdomen. Price was on his knees, straddling him, raising a short sword with a glowing tip to plunge it into Stalker's throat.

Neely screamed, "Nooooo!" Firing the blaster simultaneously, its force knocked Price off him. She ran across the grass and hit Price with a second blast, falling to her knees beside Stalker.

He was choking, trying to breathe in short gasps; a trickle of blood ran from the corner of his mouth. His eyes were open, and he met her gaze with a hint of a smile, then his eyes closed.

"Stalker," she sobbed. He couldn't die! Not now. Neely choked back another sob and looked for his weapons belt. He wasn't wearing it. Picking up the bloody sword, Neely ran back into the house. She dropped the weapon, went to the med cabinet, and grabbed a four-bolus pack of nanites.

Running back to where Stalker lay unconscious and bleeding, Neely fell to her knees. His armor had receded, and he was now wearing only a pair of shorts. She opened two nanite syringes and pumped the contents into the wound. The other two, she pumped into his nose.

"Stalker, hang on. You can't die... I love you... I need you...." Neely sobbed, putting her ear to his chest. His heart was beating slowly, and his breathing was intermittent at best.

The fact that a normal man would be dead was of little comfort. From what she'd learned of cyborg physiology, Stalker's nanites should be able to heal him. It could take hours or even days.

In the meantime, she needed help to get him into the house and secure Colton Price. And she needed to dress before they arrived. Picking up her blaster, Neely hurried into the house to their bedroom.

Opening one of her clothing drawers, she pulled out a pair of cargo shorts and a tank top and quickly donned them. Then she found her com tablet on the table by the bed and called Protector Chief Argan Shield.

"Argan, I need help. Colten Price showed up… Attacked Stalker with a lighted tip sword… Stalker is hurt bad, and I can't move him." She hurried back outside to find Coltan kneeling beside Stalker, searching for his weapon to finish him off.

Dropping her com-tablet, Neely reset her blaster to kill. "Get away from him, Colton, or I will kill you."

Colton looked up, and Neely fired off a bolt that zinged by his ear. He seemed to know that she missed on purpose and jumped up, raising his hands and backing away.

"I just came for the Mesaarkan flyer." The cyborg backed away as he spoke. "He was beating me; I had to stop him…."

"What the hell was that thing you stabbed him with?"

Colton shrugged, "A Mesaarkan radial sword. It sends a beam through the space between molecules in the armor, piercing it. Then, a radial beam cuts a circle through a few to several inches of surrounding tissue."

201

While he spoke, he was sidling around the Mesaarkan flyer parked in front of the garage. Neely raised her blaster to kill him, but Stalker gasped, drawing her attention away from Price.

When she looked back up, Colton Price was nowhere in sight. Neely wanted to check Stalker's heart and breath sounds, but she needed to know   that Colton Price wasn't circling back to attack them again and steal the Mesaarkan flyer.

A high-pitched whine in the distance announced the arrival of four protectors on hovercycles. They landed in the front yard moments later.

Only then did Neely press her ear to Stalker's chest. His heart still beat slower than normal but a little faster than before. His lungs still sounded congested, but he was breathing better.

The four cyborgs got off their hovercycles and approached Neely and Stalker. "Where's Price?" Argan asked.

"I don't know. Stalker gasped, and I looked down. Price was gone when I looked back up."

As if to answer the question, a flyer lifted off from somewhere beyond the trees that surrounded Stalker and Neely's home and grounds.

"Aren't you going after him?" Neely asked.

"Our cycles aren't fast enough to catch that power-enhanced flyer. However, I pinged it and got the ID signature. They'll track him from space and send a team after him."

"I should have killed him," Neely muttered, looking down at her fallen mate. "I used to consider him a friend… Not anymore."

"I heard Commander Dark say that some of those natural converts were never quite right after becoming cyborgs," said Argan. "Ma'am, if you could move away from the lieutenant, we'll get him into the house for you.

Neely looked up at Shield and back at Stalker. Finally, she nodded and got up, stepping back. As the four of them lifted Stalker carefully and started toward the door, she said, "Straight back to the short hallway, last door on the left."

They carried him into the bedroom and set him on his side of the bed as it was closest to the door.

"Should we get a medic for him?" Neely asked. "He seems to be hurt pretty badly."

"He was," said Argus. "I just scanned him. His internal bleeding has stopped, and the nanites are repairing the damage to his organs. It'll probably take a couple days, but he's no longer critical. I saw the nanite syringes in the grass. That was exactly what we would have done for him on the battlefield."

"Thank you for your help."

"Anytime," said Argus. "The weapon that did this to him sounds a lot like the mechanism in the rifle that nearly killed Darken's mate. She only survived because she assimilated nanites from Darken, and he added more immediately after she was shot. That bought time to get her up to the Starfire Nemesis and into a regeneration bath."

"But you don't think Stalker needs that?"

"No, he's steadily improving. I will do another scan and send it to our base medic to confirm that for you."

Argan paused to rescan Stalker and send the result to the base medic. Seconds later, her com-tablet signaled an incoming call.

One of the other cyborgs brought it to her from where she had dropped it earlier. "Neely, I agree with Protector Shield's assessment of your mate's condition. His nanites are steadily repairing the damage to his organs. It could still be a few hours before he regains consciousness. If anything changes to contradict that projection, please call me back."

Neely nodded. "I will." And ended the call.

"Do you want me to leave one of my men to guard your premises if Colton Price returns?"

Neely glanced at Stalker and frowned. She was normally adamant that she could take care of herself, but she would be distracted by Stalker's incapacitation. Even if Colton didn't come back to finish Stalker off, he might return to steal the Mesaarkan flyer.

She didn't know whether he could hack the security code to unlock it or not. But the AI would warn her if he came back. If he did, Neely would shoot to kill.

"No, thanks," she said with a smile. "The AI will warn me, and we have a whole arsenal here. After what he did to Stalker, he should think twice before returning. He only got away because Stalker was hurt, and I turned my attention away for a second. I should have blasted him."

"Don't fault yourself. It is only natural for you to be more concerned for your mate than detaining his assailant," Argan said with the right tone of sympathy. "You followed your instinct to care for your mate. He is a lucky cyborg."

"And I am lucky to have him," she said with a faint smile.

"If anything changes, call; someone can be here from the base in five minutes."

"Thanks, I will."

Chief Protector Shield inclined his head in a gesture of respect and left immediately.

Neely directed the AI to run a scan of the house and premises and lock the house once it was cleared. Then she lay on the bed beside Stalker to wait for him to awake.

Chapter Twenty-two

The room darkened, and Neely had fallen asleep, cuddled against Stalker in their bed. He moved and gave a low groan.

Neely awakened instantly and called to the AI, "Light thirty percent."

Raising herself on her side, she saw that his eyes were open, and he turned his head to meet her worried gaze.

"Stalker, honey, how do you feel?"

"Like somebody tried to gut me."

"Yeah, that bastard Colten Price."

"You were naked. I thought if I was dying, at least I got to see your tits one more time."

Neely burst out laughing. "That must be why you started to smile as you passed out."

"Fuck, I've been stabbed before, and it never hurt this bad."

"Are you in pain? Do you need some meds?" Neely asked, stroking his cheek tenderly.

"No, it's not that bad now, but when that blade went into me through my armor, I knew I was in trouble. This horrific pain ripped through my gut like an explosion inside me." Stalker took a shuddery breath, remembering. "Never felt that magnitude of pain in all those years at war, and I got shot, stabbed, and blown up so many times...."

"Four hundred eighty-seven times."

"I'm impressed that you remember."

"I remember because it hurt my heart to know you had been badly injured so many times."

"I'd do it all again if I knew you'd be waiting for me at the end."

"Oh, Stalker, I love you that much, too." She leaned over and kissed his lips lightly.

Stalker stopped her before she pulled away and drew her back for a more thorough kiss.

"Now, that's more like it," he whispered as he ended the kiss and sighed. "I've never felt this weak before. I need to eat. Those nanites devoured all my reserves to repair me."

"Whatever you want, sweetheart." Neely stroked his forehead.

"I think just some of that chocolate protein pudding. My gut still feels a little sore."

"Okay, that sounds pretty good. I forgot to eat today, and now that we're talking food, I am hungry too."

As she left the room, Stalker sat up slowly and put his feet on the floor while he calculated if he had the strength to make it to the bathroom. Taking a couple breaths and letting them out, he pushed himself to stand. The pain in his abdomen increased as gravity pulled on his internal organs. He pressed his hand to the faint mark on his belly and slowly walked ten feet to the bathroom.

He almost made it back to the bed before Neely returned with two bowls of pudding and glasses of cold tea.

"You should have told me you needed to get up. I would have helped you," she admonished.

He gave her a determined look.

"Mm Hm. Of course, you wanted to do it yourself."

She waited while he propped his pillow against the headboard and seated himself back on the bed. Neely set the tray on his lap and took her pudding and tea off, leaving Stalker with the tray.

Stalker ate silently, savoring the sweet, creamy chocolate disguising the rejuvenating ingredients. He'd eaten a lot of it during the war, and it was comfort food that made him feel better after being injured yet again. Almost as soon as he finished, he began to feel sleepy again.

He handed his tray to Neely, and she set it on the bedside table as Stalker slid down, pulling his pillow into place. He drifted to sleep almost immediately, lying on top of the covers.

Neely continued eating, watching the rise and fall of Stalker's chest. He breathed easily with no abnormal sounds. His face was in peaceful repose. Tears pricked her eyes as the horror of Colton's attack replayed in her mind, and she realized how nearly she'd lost him.

She blinked away her tears and chastised herself for dwelling on what might have been. Stalker was alive and healing. Their life together would continue, and she was grateful.

Neely had slept too much during the day to sleep more when the sun had barely set.

Covering Stalker with a light sheet, she left him alone in the bedroom to sleep.

She took her com-tablet to the living room and sat on the couch to call her mother. It had been a while, and she just needed someone to talk to.

"Hi, Mom. Are you too busy to talk?"

"Not for you, sweetie. How's life with your handsome cyborg?"

"Mostly great. Not so great today." Neely went on to relate the events of that morning. "A few seconds later, and I would have lost him."

"But he's going to be, okay?"

"Yes, he's sleeping now."

"What if Price comes back? Are you safe?"

"Our AI security system will warn us. If he comes back, my blaster won't be set on stun."

"He was always so polite when he came here. I don't know what got into him."

"You're telling me! He shot down my flyer, killed Devlin White, and he's involved with trafficking humans to the Mesaarkans."

"Oh, my!"

211

"There's no proof, but I wonder if Devlin sold Price's wife to the Mesaarkans. Colton made the rounds to all the overlords up and down East Coast investigating. Knowing how desperate he was to find her, I'm sure he didn't just ask if they knew anything. He would have looked in the back rooms and gone through the harems."

"She is either dead or off-world. After she learned Colton was coming home to her, Tessa did not go voluntarily," Vanessa said.

"Part of me feels sorry for his loss; the other part wants to end him for trying to kill Stalker."

"You really love him, don't you?"

"Yes, and you told me so." Neely chuckled. "I know he's a tough cyborg who can normally take care of himself. But I have his back."

"Have you thought about children yet?"

Neely knew that was coming. "We've talked about it for the future in a few years when my implant runs out."

"That makes sense. You need time to be a couple before you become parents. I'm sorry to hear that Stalker was hurt, but I am so glad you found each other."

"Ah, me too, Mom. I can't imagine life without him."

"Well, honey, I have to get back to work. We'll talk again soon."

"Okay, I'll be in touch."

After ending the conversation with her mother, Neely returned to the bedroom with her tablet and undressed for bed. She had slept in the nude most of her adult life and only stopped when she first shared Stalker's bed until she'd accepted him as her mate.

It seemed as though she had known him so much longer than the months since they became a couple. Now, she couldn't imagine her life without him.

Sitting in bed beside her sleeping mate, she perused the Enclave network, watching a few videos on their various restoration projects. It was easy to lose track of time, especially watching the personal stories in the public forum.

After a couple hours, she was finally ready to sleep, and she slid down in the bed, cuddling spoon fashion against her mate as he had turned on his side facing away from her. She needed to feel his warm body against her and hear his breathing and the beating of his heart. It was the reassurance she needed that finally allowed sleep to come.

When Stalker woke, Neely was cuddled in his arms, spoon fashion with her back to his front, one hand cupping her breast and the other on her mound. Of course, his cock was hard. Since he met her, there had not been many mornings that he didn't wake up hard for her.

He drew in a deep breath and no longer felt any twinge from his injury. He was completely healed and ready for action. Neely wouldn't mind if he woke her with pleasure. She actually seemed to like it.

Stalker began kneading her breast, sliding a finger into her folds, slowly stroking her clit. He plucked her nipple into a stiff peak and rolled it between his fingers and thumb.

Neely moaned and tilted her pelvis toward the finger, caressing her clit. That encouraged Stalker to start kissing her neck.

"Mm, I see we are feeling much better this morning." She hadn't missed the sensation of his hard cock laying between her butt cheeks. "Whatever you want, sweetheart… I am yours."

"I have you right where I want you," He murmured in her ear, dipping his finger inside her wet opening. His long finger went deep, caressing her g-spot, and Neely cooed. Lubricated with her juice, Stalker went back to rubbing her clit.

He wanted her to fall apart in his arms before he took pleasure for himself... To give her all the satisfaction, he knew how to give because she was everything to him.

The constant stimulation of her clit and nipple brought Neely her first orgasm of the morning. She cried out as the first wave hit her, followed by inarticulate sounds of pleasure as Stalker skillfully teased her through it. He stroked, and a wave of contractions shook her while he paused until it was over, and he stroked her again.

Chapter Twenty-three

Stalker just held her, his forearm across her breasts and hand buried in her mons, and Neely basked in the afterglow of her release. She eventually turned in his arms to face him for their first kiss of the day.

Looking at his handsome face, love for her sparkling in his midnight eyes, she couldn't fathom how she ever thought she could walk away from him. He only had to look at her like that, and she wanted to give him everything.

They kissed again, their tongues caressing and swirling in a sensual dance, sending new frissons of desire straight to her clit. He rolled her on her back, still kissing her, with his thigh between her legs against her mons.

Stalker seemed bent on a slow excursion, kissing and tasting every inch of her body. Neely knew she would be mad for release before he finished, but she didn't mind because she knew it would be mind-blowing when it came.

He made a thorough tour of her neck and upper chest before reaching her throbbing nipples, sucking each one at length. Then it was on to her lower chest and abdomen.

Neely was a quivering mass before he even reached her mons. He spread her legs and pushed them up, so her feet were flat on the bed. He dragged his tongue up her channel lapping her juices before his lips settled on her clit. She was so wet then, he easily pushed two fingers inside her.

The sheer delight was excruciating, and Neely didn't last long before screaming in ecstasy with the sheer magnitude of her orgasm. Each time he lapped his tongue over her clit she bucked her hips, clawing at the bed and crying out at his sweet torment.

Soon he was kissing and tasting his way back up her body until they were face to face. "Are you ready," he asked sweetly after a tender kiss.

"I am so ready!" she asserted. "I love you."

"And I love you," he whispered huskily, then kissed her again. Seconds later, his cock was filling her.

Neely was happy to let him set the pace; she wanted him to feel the exquisite pleasure he'd given her. Thrust after thrust, he pounded into her faster and faster, slamming his cock hard and deep into her.

217

She reveled in his carnal onslaught. His passion seemed to stoke hers even higher. This cyborg man was the one she loved beyond all doubt, more than she ever dreamed possible.

As they chased their mutual climax, it was as if the world fell away, and they rose onto their own cloud, soaring in ecstasy until she came again and brought him with her. Neely cried out in joy as his cock pulsed inside her, pumping his hot seed into her womb where one day it would take hold, and their child would grow.

But not today. Today was just for them to share their love through their joining. And it was a great day to be alive.

Two days later, a ten-man cyborg team arrived to demolish standing structures to make way for the new town. They brought counselors to liaise with the dwellers living in partial buildings that provided a modicum of shelter.

They had learned a lot since Vyken Dark, and his team had returned to Earth five years ago. As soon as the demolitions were finished, the next crew arrived with machinery to clear away the rubble and prepare the ground for rebuilding.

A small town soon replaced the section of Los Angeles once ruled by Vradin Blackwood. New homes were spaced widely apart to give residents room to homestead. While the rescued people were in the refuge, Enclave advisors taught them how to grow their own fruits and vegetables and preserve them.

That was just the start. Initially, the Enclave would continue sending supplies to keep the citizens fed and clothed while working toward self-sufficiency. The Enclave also encouraged cottage industries such as weaving cloth from cotton and making clothing, soap making, and milling grains.

Medics collected DNA from women who wanted to find a cyborg mate, while several found their males by chance. By the time Neely's new friend Rena moved into her new home, she had accepted Brandix as her mate.

Word spread throughout the region as the first new town was built and settled. It was something tangible that people could see. Many were eager to cooperate once people living in broken-down buildings realized they could live in decent houses and receive food, clothing, and tools to become self-sufficient.

Renovating the former Los Angeles megalopolis was one of the biggest jobs in re-taming the west. Stalker was grateful that gang bosses there didn't have the Federation in their pocket like the eastern Overlords. That gave him freer rein to apply the law equally and earned him a reputation for being tough but fair.

Limited access to machinery for clearing the ruins and construction of new housing made overall progress slower than optimal. They needed to build more factories, to build the machinery required to build more factories.

It would come, and the cyborgs were determined to make it happen because they had a big stake in making it a good place to nurture their mates and raise their offspring. But it would take time.

Epilogue

Four years later

It was 3 a.m., and the baby was crying. Stalker jumped out of bed and scooped his son Jarrod from his crib before his crying woke Neely. At least he'd slept long enough for his parents' uninterrupted lovemaking.

Stalker smiled to himself as he cuddled his son against his shoulder, carrying him to the kitchen to extract a bottle of breast milk from the refrigerator. He warmed it to body temperature in seconds in the food processor, then carried his tiny boy to the living room to feed him.

Needing far less sleep than an unenhanced human, it was no hardship for Stalker to tend to his beautiful son in the middle of the night, even multiple times. Stalker relished his time with his tiny son as he watched him suckle his mother's milk from the bottle.

Even though he knew the biology, the reality of creating another life with his beloved mate seemed nothing short of miraculous. That two people could fill his life with so much love was more than he ever dared to dream.

The End

Thank you for reading our book Stalker, Cyborg Ranger. If you enjoyed reading it, please let us know by leaving a review.

Clarissa Lake
Christine Myers

About the Authors

Clarissa Lake grew up watching Star Trek and reading Marvel Comics. She attended science fiction and fantasy conventions where she met many well-known science fiction authors and attended their readings and discussion panels. They included scifi greats Anne McCaffery, CJ Cherry, George RR Martin, Ben Bova, Timothy Zahn, Frederik Pohl, Orson Scot Card.

After years of fruitless efforts to get her books published traditionally, she discovered Kindle Direct Publishing and became an Indie author-publisher.

While she loves scifi, she always thought there should be more romance so she started writing it hot and steamy.

Christine Myers has been a science fiction fan since seeing the original "Day the Earth Stood Still" at age eight. Her favorite subgenre is science fiction romance with interstellar space travel and a bit of space opera. Among the most influential in her work are the Lazarus Long novels by Robert Heinlein including "Time Enough for Love", and Marta Randall's "Journey." She loves

Star Trek, Firefly, Farscape, and Veteran Cosmic Rockers, the Moody Blues.

After spending years trying to get her work published by traditional publishers, she discovered KDP and became an Indie Author/Publisher. This means she does it all from writing to publishing.

Previous Cyborg Books

Cyborg Awakenings: Prequel

by Christine Myers (Author)

Every major city on Earth has been destroyed by the Mesaarkan's in revenge for a massacre on a distant colony by an Earth survey team. Cyborgs have been created by the thousands to fight the hundred-year war. While the fighting continues on alien worlds, survivors and their descendants struggle to subsist in what was once Chicago. They live in ruined buildings without utilities or running water, much like the pioneers in the 19th century.

Vyken Dark: Cyborg Awakenings Book One

by Christine Myers (Author)

Cyborg Vyken Dark is back on Earth after fighting for eighty years in the Procyon War against the Mesaarkans. He came to help restore order out of chaos in old Chicago, USA. Every major city on Earth is in ruins. Most are now run by gangs of thugs ruled by overlords who take everything of value and prey on those just trying to survive. Vyken and his four brother cyborgs are all that's left of their starship crew of three hundred.

He didn't want the job, but when his old mentor Admiral Carson Gregor asked, Vyken Dark could not refuse. If he could have chosen a man to call father, it would have been Carson Gregor.

Vyken chose the name Dark because the darkness in his soul drove him to kill the enemies of the Federation with a ruthlessness that few natural humans possessed. Sometimes that darkness overwhelmed his humanity and made him weary of his life... Until he came back to Earth and found her.

Jolt Somber (Cyborg Awakenings Book 2)

by Christine Myers (Author), Clarissa Lake (Author), T.J. Quinn (Author)

Jolt Somber was the name the cyborg picked for himself. He was created to be a killer, and his creators reinforced his killer instinct by flooding him with feel-good endorphins. For eighty years, he fought the Mesaarkans at Vyken Dark's side. He and four genetic cyborg brothers returned to Earth to help restore civilization after the war had ended.

Jolt is supervising demolition in the ruins of Farringay to build a new starport. The war left Earth in ruins with cities ruled by overlords with gangs of thugs as enforcers. Violence against women is rampant.

When Jolt finds his one genetic female mate used and left for dead by gangers, the pleasure he takes in avenging her could have unexpected repercussions.

After what males had done to her, would she ever accept Jolt as her mate?

Talia's Cyborg (Cyborg Awakenings Book 3)

by Clarissa Lake (Author), Christine Myers (Author)

The interstellar war left Earth in ruins. After the war, cyborgs returned to rebuild and restore civilization and began awakening the cyborgs still in stasis, waiting to fight.

Talia Cannon, a descendant of apocalypse preppers, lives on a small, off-grid homestead in the Blue Ridge Mountains. She is the last of her family line unless she finds a mate.

Jolt Somber has learned that building families is one way to rebuild civilization. So, he takes Talia to Farringay to see if one of the cyborgs under his command is her male, her genetically matched soulmate.

Bodee Flint, nearly the last cyborg she meets, is the one. One passionate kiss tells her this hot young cyborg is for her, but what about love? Then again, he's sexy and thoughtful, and he adores her. What's not to love? Whenever Talia has sexy thoughts, Bodee is ready and willing to breed to make offspring. He is the best thing that ever happened to her.But will she realize what he means to her before it's too late?

This book is for adult audiences and contains explicit sexual encounters.

Axel Rex (Cyborg Awakenings Book 4)

by Clarissa Lake (Author), Christine Myers

One of the thousands of cyborgs produced for the interstellar war with the Mesaarkans, Axel Rex remained in stasis throughout the war. He supervises the demolition of several square kilometers of ruins in Farringay to make way for a new interstellar starport. He was educated and trained as a warrior during his virtual life in stasis. He was also prepared for love if he found the one genetically-compatible female with whom he could breed and make offspring. The chance for a family of his own and freedom at the end of service motivated them to serve.

Axel is too busy supervising 500 cyborgs to daydream about finding love at the demolition site. Then one stubborn female refuses to leave a building set for demolition.

Layna Rose lived with her cat Sammy in the ruins of Farringay and had claimed a ruined apartment building as a home. No cyborg goon will make her give up her home until Axel pulls her out, kicking and screaming.

She pleads with him to let her go back for her cat. Layna takes the opportunity to grab her cat and run. Axel intercepts her quickly and suspects she is his genetic match. He convinces her to go back to the barracks with him for food, shelter, and new clothing. While they are eating, he tells her she is his match.

She thinks he just wants her for sex, and she doesn't quite believe he wants her to be his mate for life. But the food is good, and it's nice to be clean and have new clothing. Layna can't deny the primal sexual attraction she feels for Axel. Not even sure she likes him, she knows she won't get a better offer. Bedding Axel is no hardship, but Layna doesn't delude herself; they are in love. Could she love a cyborg? Could she love this cyborg? Sexually explicit for adults. Guaranteed HEA.

Dagger Jack (Cyborg Awakenings Book 5)

by Clarissa Lake (Author), Christine Myers (Author)

Dagger Jack is a spinoff novella about a peripheral character introduced in Axel Rex. He was left clinically dead with catastrophic injuries sustained in an ambush by rogue cyborgs.

When he was awakened at the cyborg production facility south of Chicago, his life was mapped out for him. After he helped rebuild a city and a starport destroyed during an interstellar war, he would become a Protector in one of the rural communities reclaimed from the overlords in the east.

231

When he awakens the second time, he doesn't want to be a protector. Just before he went down, he scented his female. He wants to go back to find her before he has fully recovered.

He was made for war, but only her love would make him whole again.

Note: *This book can be read as a standalone, but reading the previous books in the series will enhance reading this story.*

Re-edited and revised with preview chapters of **Blaze, Cyborg Ranger**, *Book One of the Cyborg Rangers Series* set in the *Cyborg Awakenings* universe.

Blaze: Cyborg Ranger (Cyborg Rangers Series Book 1)

Clarissa Lake (Author), Christine Myers (Author)

Blaze Savage, a cyborg marine ranger, fought in an interstellar war for ninety years. Captured and tortured by the enemy, he had wished for death in the darkest times.

The promise of *her,* the one female who was his genetic complement with whom he could breed and make a family, kept him from giving up. It was the promise of love embedded in their programming. But there was no plan for the cyborgs' happy ending when the war was over.

After the war, Blaze went to the cyborg planet Phantom, needing time to decompress. But he knew he wouldn't find her on a world with hardly any females.

When Commander Vyken Dark needed a team of rangers to bring law and order to the west, Blaze was ready to start the next part of his life on Earth, where he is already in the database of females looking for cyborg mates.

But fate steps in, and Blaze finds her running from a man who claims she belongs to him…

WARNING: This book is a sizzling Sci-fi Romance with multiple explicit sex scenes and the mention of rape. It also contains incidents of graphic violence. If these are triggers for you, please do not buy or read this book.

Darken: Cyborg Ranger (Cyborg Rangers Series Book 2

Darken Wolf, former second in command in his Cyborg Marine Ranger team, learns his genetic mate is found while going to Earth to become a law enforcement ranger in the post-apocalyptic American West. When he arrives to meet her, he learns she is missing.

Gina Malcolm's best friend points him to Overlord Devlin White, who she escaped from several years before. Darken steals into the Overlord's compound to free her, and they flee. Of course, it couldn't be that easy.

A fighter plane follows Darken's sky cycle and shoots them down over the New Mexican desert. While the landing was a little rough, the bigger problem is that Darken's CPU shuts down, and the sky cycle burns along with Darken's only comm. He is not even sure where they are but decides going North is the best plan. It could be a very long walk.

This is only the beginning as they get acquainted and embark on a life as a couple. All they have to do is survive long enough to share a future together.

Printed in Great Britain
by Amazon